The Great Awakening

"Remembering the Sacred Music"

O7734

VIE Loriot de Rouvray

Copyright©2025 by VIE Loriot de Rouvray

ISBN: 979-8-9905885-3-0 PB
ISBN: 979-8-9905885-4-7 HB

All rights reserved.

No part of this book may be reproduced or transmitted in any form
or by any means, electronic or mechanical, including
photocopying, recording, or by any information storage and
retrieval system, without permission in writing from the copyright
owner.

The views expressed in this work are solely those of the author.

Independently Published by VIE Loriot de Rouvray

"Oneness"
With
CHADD & VIE

The God
Duo Radiating Light
(Victorious in Christ)

I dedicate this book to my blue flame

And I would like to express my gratitude to Blessed Mother Mary undoer of knots, the Ambassador Asuba, the Light beings from the sixth dimension to Father Damien, Wanda Harmon, Elyse Parakero, to my ancestor and guide Elesteau, Saint Aloysius, and to Saint Michael the Archangel.

*"Les esprits forts
discutent des idees, les
esprits moyens discutent
des evenements, les esprits
faibles discutent
des gens."*

(Socrate)

"Remembering
The Sacred Music"
Christ Consciousness

"Whistleblowers and awakened people are always taken for lunatics or conspirators, but in the end, they are the ones always proven to be right."

And God said, "Let there be Light; and there was light. And God saw the light, that it was good: and God divided the light from the darkness." Genesis 1:3-13

If you want to find the Key to the universe, think in terms of energy, frequency, and vibration - Nikola Tesla

-

"We came before you to stand behind you.."

CHADD Ghostwriter

NOTE FOR READERS

"Awareness of Ignorance is the beginning of wisdom" -Aristotle

Each of my books is a different and unique experience that will reshape your understanding of reality, spirituality, and the Self. It takes you on a spiritual journey for your growth and well-being, which are powerful steps to personal growth and self-transformation. They should be read in chronological sequence.

These books are written quite differently, they are understanding of humankind's reality. It will allow much more quickly. It's encoded in the books to open up the consciousness.

The readers of these books act as a bridge between human awakenings, it will change the way you will make you understand your motivation.

- 9.1.1. Complete Guide To Natural Healing (Book 1) (This book was guided by the Archangel Michael)
- Destiny of the Dog; Beware of The Almighty (volume 1)
- Time is Ticking; The Fifth Amendment (volume 2)
- Karma Through The Window of Time (Volume 3)
- New Century, New Era, New Experiences (volume 4)
- Intonex (Volume 5)

- The Genome of The Ancient Creators "ABBA EBEN" (volume 6)
- The Phoenix with the Crystal Plumage (volume 7)
- The Great Awakening; Remembering the Sacred Music (volume 8)
- 9..1.1. Aroma Essential Therapy (Book 2)

INTRODUCTION

Buckle up for an unequaled journey. You have chosen to be here. This book, The Great Awakening carries within it higher levels of consciousness as the quest to find your path and purpose continues. The healing energy from this information is very powerful, the book and the energy associated with the information.

My name is VIE. I am your guide into the Light. Finding your way is not an easy task, and we the God Duo had to go through traumatic physical and mental pain to deliver you the hidden truth. Our bodies have been attacked with poison and beaten. CHADD Baker acted many times and for years. He had to undergo a coma, a heart attack, and surgeries due to beatings, assaults, and poisons. I was attacked many times on various parts of my body by dark souls practicing magic spells and voodoo. By some lost souls who worship Lucifer and would not like to see the God Duo reunited and working together.

The GOD DUO, in this series of books for expansion of mind, are two warriors of GOD. A couple of Archangels on Earth were chosen and sent to help you by the highest Government of the Universe. They are both in-life Doctors, CHADD is the Dr. of Sound and VIE is the Dr. of Light. They have created some music, VIE is the writer of these books. CHADD is the ghostwriter, and they own the instituteoflightandsound.com

Once again, I am bringing you some information in this book that in my opinion and my understanding is real. But I am asking you to use your intuition and discernment.

All of you are here as you know by now for a reason. Your memories were erased by the Dark Entities a long time ago. Everyone who resides as a human on this planet comes from different Star Systems, Galaxies, and Universes. You made a promise before arriving here to help liberate Mother Earth from the Dracos and Reptilians. The Draconians were actually, a militant race that was carrying out orders from above. In most Galactic histories, there are records of the Draco-Lyran war. Unfortunately, there are a lot of different versions of what really happened. Because the Lyrans weren't prepared for contact with the more advanced Draconian military. Most of what is remembered is only a vague memory of the fact.

The allies of the Draconians were purely a psychic race that had not yet found a suitable tangible form. They had a contract with the Draconians. Their allies would give the Draconians powerful training on psychic mind control and technologies; in return, the Draconians would do genetic research and farm supplies for their allies.

Now, new energies and timelines are aligning in a Divine Order to help you regain your abilities by moving into higher frequencies.

The Human race is a unique, eternal aspect of consciousness with an infinity of potential the Dark entities are after.

Everything is coming together into a perfect alignment, the human race needs to take their power and their destiny back into their own hands to free themselves from this enslavement, which lasted for too long as all of you know.

Meantime, you need to resist the New World Order, Our One World Government, on what they are trying to force on you and please, be aware that vaccines are dangerous for humans, as they contain mercury, spike protein, and nanotechnology set up to destroy the human body.

This is why it's very important to take control of your own lives now and don't wait too long as each minute is crucial for this New World. All of you have the inner strength within you to accomplish this task of freeing yourself from this 3D prison.

Your media is going to be completely dismantled for not being truthful and lying to the people and will be replaced by the truth, and there will be no more need for the mass media anymore. Old times are going to dissolve, and a new bright future will arrive.

New times are coming. The upcoming transformation that is already happening like the rescuing of many children, cult members being captured, the removal of the Dark Ones who committed crimes against the civilization, and arrests of Negative government officials. Also, no new Dark Forces can enter this planet; they are banned and are cut off by the Galactic Fleets.

Please, be prepared for your lives to change so drastically that you are going to feel like you're living in a science fiction movie. You are going to forget about your old 3D Matrix life very quickly like it never existed before, only adventures and joy are going to be part of your daily life.

5D is Heaven, a Gamma State, a blissful state.

There are 12-dimensional boundaries in this Universe. Our bodies have 12 primary strands of DNA which work like nano-sized fiber optic cables and 12 multi-dimensional chakra portals that let Akashic light data flow in and out of the body. This data is stored in our cellular memory. This information alone should tell you just how incredibly powerful we truly are.

Ten of these DNA strands were deactivated eons ago by these Dark rulers, but they are now activated, and this is changing the entire game. Most Starseeds on this planet right now have between four and five of these strands activated.

The old low-vibrating 3D Earth Matrix is one state of consciousness and the new 5D matrix is a faster-vibrating state of consciousness.

The human population is now finding out that a group of dark, nefarious beings has controlled humanity and Earth by deception. The reason for the cover-up of our entire existence is that our energy could be harvested lifetime after lifetime. This incredible amount of energy has been harvested and redirected for their use.

Unconscious humans are so asleep and so far gone at this point in regard to what is truly happening it's irrelevant to be so concerned for their Ascension, There is nothing that can be done to help them until they are ready. Until humans stop hurting and killing each other there is no immediate solution for them. So, it is wise for you to keep your focus on your progression at this moment.

The Ascension Event is going to come up on the humans very quickly and abruptly and the Pleiadians know that most are not prepared for it and are trying to make this transition as painless as possible.

Incredible amounts of high-frequency gamma Photon Light is penetrating Earth in the last 6 months or so. These frequencies, these levels of light have been secretly measured by every space agency on this planet and are completely hidden from us.

These space agencies are hiding, trying to anyway, the hundreds of thousands of Extra-Terrestrial craft that are being seen around the sun this is the very reason solar observatories were shut down trying not to leak photos and video of these massive armadas of craft and vessels. However, the Pleiadians did agree with this shutdown because they knew a huge majority of humanity was not ready for such a blunt disclosure yet.

The solar event is nearby. The question is are you ready? Is your body prepared to receive that much frequently?

The Great Solar Flash Event is coming, and It is going to be the most incredible thing we have ever experienced!

Some people might be scared or skeptical, but it isn't some conspiracy theory. Whether you believe it or not, very shortly, a powerful energy surge will be released into our system!

Be prepared for this great event with hope and optimism to look forward to a new world and a new era of peace and harmony. To a new understanding of the human place in the Universe. Be ready for it!

SYNOPSIS

Every night as VIE continues to get dreams, visions, and visitations, she is helped by entities from other realms and aliens. She and her blue flame then embark on a new thrilling adventure to live with other people in another realm. When she astral travels and meets them she receives crucial information and answers from star sisters or spiritual people from different realms.

Even though the situation on the surface may seem chaotic, the planet has been in the Galactic Federation's hands for several months now.

The Pleiadian fleet is waiting in the skies looking at the Starseeds mentally creating Golden pillars of peace at their respective location on the surface and downloading the Care Packages through them. This will finally bring the supplies to their intended destination.

Big changes are coming. The world's lakes, oceans, rivers, and waterways will be restored to purity, as well as soil and farmland. Using toxic chemicals on foods will cease, and pharmaceutical companies will be dismantled. Holistic practices will take over and will be the norm. Governments will be eradicated, and the people of each nation will govern themselves. Clean energy will be utilized. Hospitals will be equipped with new alternative and holistic technology like med beds and therapies and treatments.

This odyssey began when VIE met CHADD in a wheelchair and felt a deep and strong connection, inexplicable. She got to know him better and became enveloped in a world of mysticism, government conspiracies, religions/cults, and upcoming prophesied events. Entered a world of lies deception, hope, and pain. Her spiritual journey began when she joined forces with her blue flame, CHADD, to bring the words of Jesus.

Henri was a professor who lived near an Indian tribal reservation and had a son, Edward, with his wife, Martha. Edward married Ethel, and they had a son CHADD, who was diagnosed with several behaviors and mental problems after his dad took him to the government hospital that his father, Edward, used at the request of the NSA. At the age of five, they started to do testing on CHADD to understand his unique ability. Though he was never sick, CHADD was given multiple drugs at the age of five. Then Edward divorced, and during Edward and Ethel's separation, he started dating a coworker named Katherine, an archon known as the harsh woman, or surnamed the Surrogate, working hand in hand with CHADD's half-brother, Paul. Katherine's son, Paul, was a sworn law enforcement officer then. Paul, Carlos, and Katherine were all involved with the corrupt government. The government would take the drugs from the drug dealers in the West, send them to Miami for sale in Florida, and generate money for the government's clandestine operations.

CHADD spent time in hospitals and medical centers, and during his stay in the hospital, a group called Guardians revealed themselves. They were the Cathari. There were two elements to them, the Perfecti and the Believers. The Perfecti were helpful and wanted to bring people closer to God. They defeated Hitler. The Believers were the Nazis and are the serial killers of today and the many world leaders that destroyed rather than created. Extremely intelligent and hypnotizing at the same time, some of the Believers had guidance in genetic reproduction thousands of years ago, before and after the great flood, to create creatures seen throughout history as vampires, werewolves, Bigfoot, and reptilians.

CHADD is a baker act drugged up a ward of the state, holds the keys to the Divine wisdom, and with VIE brings humanity into the light of God just when it all seems lost. But all of this was a treat to the Anunnaki who wanted the Earth for themselves. So, they manipulated the story of Christ, in order, to be successful with the takeover of Earth...A never-ending battle of good and evil: the modern world is a literal and figurative warzone.

The straightest path to the truth is to expose all information that is officially forbidden.

The secret Government controls the population through false information Christ was a healer; He worked with the emotional body, and He resurrected from the dead. The Church stripped away the virility of Christ by hiding His true relationship with Marie-Madeleine, and the male was emasculated and the female denied.

Illuminati's are in key places and all institutions are corrupted. Their agenda is to reduce the population and to manipulate humanity keeping them under their control through drugs, flu, antibiotic shots, implanted diseases, weather catastrophes, and wars.

The Thuggees medical doctors from India reincarnated and infiltrated every hospital in the state. They keep CHADD by court orders, in drugs, and in a foggy state between Mental Hospitals and asylums. They shot him with dangerous drugs, brainwashed, programmed then manipulated him, in the land of freedom…. They sent an Asian couple to steal the Vajra from VIE after putting some drugs in her drink. She has been poisoned more than once, they invaded her body with alien parasites, crippled her hands and her feet, and much more. They were projecting to kill her by targeting her heart.

Jesus and Mary-Madeleine are returning to demonstrate the path of Oneness and Divine Love. To awaken new frequencies within One's being, defragment old programming that no longer serves so that humanity can embrace the Light and Sound of creation to expand consciousness.

Christ delivered His bloodline, and His star codes, through the Goddess (Marie-Madeleine) and He brought the ultimate creativity that could transmute human violence: The Eucharist" true Christ.

There is a powerful message brought to the world, and it is about the Matrix and the Ascension process to reach the Golden Age with warnings and future predictions that you may or may not want to hear but have to hear.

Once you'll remember your multidimensionality then Christ will awaken in you. And it is Time! The Golden Age is within reach.

CHADD & VIE have the knowledge that can be used to enlighten your world and help resolve the difference that separates you on Earth.

"Henri the Professor, and CHADD's grandfather has now passed away from Alzheimer's after being found lost in a hospital hallway from a heart attack. Edward, CHADD's father died after a long battle against diabetes II. Katherine has now diabetes II after eating a bad diet, her son Paul has cancer and the nephew hacks computers for a living for the cabal. The three hybrids don't have much time left to live on Earth as they have found a way to separate CHADD and VIE."

While CHADD is kept on drugs VIE is helped and guided by entities from other realms and Aliens. It's about an illegal program to experiment with mind control initiated by the CIA. How the moon influences life on Earth. The UN thought to eliminate all borders and genders to create an atheist human field human race since they realized that Christianity was based on the Essene teaching. The Roman Empire stepped in to eliminate the teachings from the Essene, the human ascension: the transformation of your body into a body of light or the rainbow body.

Other civilizations are back here to help the earth, just when the CIA & NSA target anyone, anywhere, anytime on Earth with mind control technology and program their victims entraining the brain to their remote neural monitoring system while blaming the population for Global warming that they create.

Be Careful. There is no ascension without Spirituality or Divine Reconnection, and when you awaken and become a serious co-creator, the cabal will have no more power to rule the world. But you have to make it. Watch out for Gurus, false prophets, and cults.

Christ will come down from revolving Light clouds with a multitude of Masters gathered around him. Many will be glad, and many will be sorrowful at the sight, for they did not recognize that their Masters were in the midst, walking among the Earth.

It is the ability to enrich the world through the journey of the mystics, the universal voyage. Each individual has to travel in their own time for it reveals the path of knowledge and transcends time and space. This path reveals the higher truth of personal evolution that you are invited to find.

The teaching of Jesus Christ is essential in respect to the awakening happening now. It is teaching entirely based on love and respect for each other. Non-believers in God are used for mind control or real demonic possession. The fallen angels, the Illuminati, have abused the physical creations. The archons are inorganic and artificial and make a bad copy of our original reality. The

Illuminati want a one-world government, and they selected electronics to be brought to Planet Earth for that and to keep control of humans. The pineal gland is the key to ascension and the higher vibration, and the cabal does not want you to regenerate it.

Once the regeneration process begins, they won't be able to stop it. (there is no need for children 's transfusion blood) People will no longer be susceptible to control human beings on the planet. What if the Library of Alexandria was the link to today's affliction of the world and the Cabal? The Templars fought the forces of Islam in Spain and on the sunbaked hills where Jesus lived and died. The knowledge that the Cabal has in sacred geometry forms to control and create a single government. But the new template is here. The New Tools for the New Earth.

The falling away from power and the manipulation that stimulates life forms that are unevolved into finding something better. So, there is a great benefit in this whole process and nothing to be frightened of. Absolutely nothing. There is absolutely nothing to fear in these times that are coming. As you begin to honor yourself, you will draw to yourself opportunities beyond your conception.

There is power and importance in the numbers, the colors, the light, the sound frequencies, and the vibration related to our health and why it has been hidden from you. And there is also power in the frequency vibration of a number that is the anti-New World Order.

PROLOGUE

This book is written as an initiation for you to hold the intention of empowering you to be a co-player on planet Earth.

"The Great Awakening" is built upon insight while times of political corruption and financial instability are growing, launching a spiritual adventure that will transform all who take the journey. The intense power of synchronicity and spiritual purpose blends the adventure with the real insight and visions that the characters encounter. With a curse that has been put as obstacles to the couple called the God Duo Warriors, CHADD and VIE. CHADD is the Messenger of God and VIE is the door to the Divine.

I am assuming that by the time you found this book, you were now familiar with my work, and how I began to write and obtain information.

In my work as a writer and a Visionary transformative energy healer, speaking the language of the light for soul activation, I felt a strong desire to write about the importance of the opening of consciousness. The Holy Spirit made me shift the stagnant energy for the entire planet. It's a field that works through all times and realms. I was guided to take responsibility and duty for creating a peaceful world.

My name is VIE. I am a teacher and a healer. It is a gift from God, wisdom. I have been chosen to be your door to the Divine. CHADD holds the key to Divine wisdom. We are CHADD and I the God Duo victorious in Christ.

Although I have been chosen to be your door to the divine, or because I have been chosen to reconnect with you, heal you and bring you knowledge by those in need of my experience and knowledge, I am fighting these dark and nasty entities to be located, found and discovered by them lately. And here I say to them, Oh! No! Careful! stop doing what you are doing you do not want to be confronted with my high vibration again. Stop immediately and run as fast as you can. Remember a few years ago at the Body, Mind, Spirit expo? I was very patient with you until you had a taste of my high vibration. You could not stand it. So, keep it in mind.

We have been Judged and labeled with many crazy names while the Dark energies in control and their hybrid archons tried everything to separate us, and many times tried to kill us both. We are here on a "Humanitarian Mission", and we prefer to be named conspirators than their partners in crime.

How can we possibly explain to unprepared, unopened-minded, and unawakened people around us, relatives, acquaintances, or friends, how can we disclose and make them understand the meeting, the reunion, of two angels with one common mission on earth? How can we explain to the people who had their software of life hacked by vaccination and then programmed by the elites in control? We are here to help people on Earth, also known as Terra Christa.

And what would you do to make them understand I was also contacted and trained by Archangel Michael, who will later join and help me?

When He appeared to me He was wearing a T-shirt and a short like any other human being. He did not look anything like you might have imagined for a Divine being. But yes, he was sitting next to me with his beautiful blue eyes and introduced himself and said: "What name can you give me? I have two wings on my back. I am here to help you"

While CHADD was poisoned again by a cook in a mental hospital, they took the opportunity of surgery on his esophagus and installed a mesh. That took place when Katherine went to visit him with some cookies. He is now losing weight because he has a hard time swallowing his food.

Me? They forced me to do three COVID tests in less than a week so that the dark energies could break the barrier of what served as an obstacle to all forms of pollution in my nose and infested me with a horrible virus. A sort of a plague.

Without the help of our spiritual friends behind the veil, we would not have been able to make it and continue our humanitarian mission. The pineal gland is a key to the invisible, and in Egypt, that was a punishment for slaves. It is an attack on the pineal gland, the breaking of the gland of blood encephalitis.

The hematoencephalitis gland separates the false nasal hollow from the mondanta gollow and serves as an obstacle to all forms of pollution, viruses, and bacteria. The blood-brain barrier is a layer of cells that protect the brain from heavy metals, pesticides and other toxic substances. The damage that will follow can be irreversible.

Emerging from my dream I remembered that one night when an angel-like figure came into the room through the wall. There was something very interesting about her. She had this mystical vibe. She was wearing a long skirt and had many pieces of jewelry. Her skin was smooth and beautiful. She smiled at me and began to speak.

I was given the task of informing humans about a Digit number. One numerical digit symbol stops the agenda and transforms the world. This frequency vibration has been blocked on purpose by dark energies. The number seven is the anti-New World Order.

It's the secret of getting the world out of Covid. For that reason, seven is called a lucky number. It's one of the things that will transform people from being vaccinated, and it is a protection against the dark. This COVID "vaccination" contains micro microbes AI in the vaccinations, and it is programmed to change the DNA with an agenda behind it.

A French scientist said: They inject a genetic code into your body! It is not a vaccine or a genetic therapy it is an injection of genetic code in healthy people that they want to be programmed. And I am here, the French Scientist says, to tell you that they are hacking the software of life. Now you will understand why they talk about "the great reinitiation". They call it "software of life," says a Doctor from a vaccine company.

Commandant Ashtar from the Galactic Federation float calls it quackcination not good for your health. And says, these v$xxin3s were created only to control you or destroy your human body with nanotechnology.

There are levels of war, and many beings have been sent to frighten you, I hear. "The surrogate that you know under the name of Katherine, says the angel that appeared, is also called the harsh woman. Her son Paul and his two daughters are archons. the grandson, the uncle and aunts like the grand-daddy that was one (now passed away and living with the dark ones on the other side of the veil) they all have always worked against you for years."

We were already an expert on the higher etheric realms and came to help, and our journey has been very down to earth so far; and painful. Our existence is multilayered and there is much going on in the background of which you are unaware. It will all be revealed in time.

Light, from one point of view, is information. As we share our light with you, we will engage in a mind-to-mind exchange to extend your field of perception, to explore the corridors of time through your DNA for you to remember the real history of your planet and yourselves. You have been taught that early humans crawled out of caves or were expelled from the garden, and they slowly evolved over a few thousand years, struggling with the ice ages and discovering the wheel. This is certainly not the case. You spring from an ancestral heritage that comes from the stars.

Your challenge currently is to gain your freedom. You are in conditional liberty under surveillance. Although it may appear as if you are being squeezed and your individuality annihilated, there is always a bigger picture. In dealing with day-to-day living, you may find yourself questioning your sanity, your purpose, and what to do from moment to moment, overwhelmed by the whole spectrum of life. We will tell you that the picture is bigger than you can imagine. Life on Earth includes much more than you thought, so do not get stressed out now, for there is much more to come. We intend to help you get through these times.

TABLE OF CONTENTS

CHAPTER 1
Visions: The Battle for Consciousness

I thought I was waking up, But I wasn't. I began to have visions appearing. and what I saw was a chess board Game and now I am seeing that what we are living in is a holographic Game. The game was set up years ago by the Freemasons, they said, with different rules. Then I saw them using the Bible, The Quran, and the Torah to set division among humans living on Earth. Then I saw the Free Masons, the Elite in power and their minions creating fights for the richest of the countries and the power to reign and govern. It is violent.

They are about the consciousness. They are after your consciousness to eliminate you, and Artificial Intelligence (AI) takes over. They enslave the population and create Wars. It creates more benefits and money. They create battles for resources like oil and Gold, silver, uranium, diamonds, etc. It's serving their agenda of reducing the population. Another opportunity for genocide.

They infiltrated everywhere in the system. In Law enforcement, Governments, the financial system, justice, medical, hospital, and financial systems. Everywhere to control and enslave the people in the world. They use advanced technologies. Chemtrail is a spray of diseases, electronics, chemicals and that poisons the body with drugs and vaccinations. Create fear to impose vaccination shots. Marking humans with the mark of the beast inserting AI to take over the source consciousness. Their goal is to replace humans.

They created Israel just to create Chaos in the world and WW III so that the population would beg for peace, and they would tell them the only way to have peace is to have a One World Government. And one man will be looked by you as the savior of the world. It will be the anti-Christ.

But nothing is frozen in time…

CHAPTER 2
The GOD DUO Came To Help You

"Pour savoir qui vous dirige, il suffit de regarder ceux que vous ne pouvez pas critiquer" Voltaire

I found myself in an enlightened state of mind. One more elevated state of mind than usual. Sent through the mirror's time I received the message of salvation and deliverance. A message of love, passion, and compassion. And I was told: "Sacred energies from the afterlife have been sent out by the Universe to look out for you...Recently, they have been sending you messages through numeric signs, but it is unclear if you have received them."

My subconscious and the Universe were also encouraging me to go forward and move in the direction of my mission to accomplish. And the message continues:

"I am your and the collective consciousness. Once upon a time, there were beings who dreamed of amassing great power, who yearned to be worshiped and feared. Earthly beings are fulfilling their fantasy by participating in this Earth reality right now. That which you call the shadow government or global elites, beings of great status and power on your planet, was once average folk in other realities who dreamed of being powerful.

They wanted the experience of superiority, of god-like status over all others within their reality. And so, there will is now being met, their fantasy is being fulfilled, and it is the love that you had for these beings that allows that to be so. They are not forcing you to submit, as it appears from your physical perspective. From a spiritual perspective, you are magnifying their light by willingly diminishing your own. This is a gift you are giving them, and it is a gift that has been given to you in past lives by others as well. You diminish your power, your intelligence, your strength, your freedom, etc., so that someone else can feel superior compared to you.

No one should have to live with the constant fear of war or apocalyptic end times, which is why we must heal the universe, beginning especially with the nexus points. You have agreed to transmute yourselves, to ascend and return to harmonious balance among yourselves.

The Crown of the Cosmos has chosen the path of light. And this is exciting for us, your spiritual family, very much.

As we dive deeper into the Aquarian Age, the voice continues, the negative murmurs in minds are now easier to detect and the body sculpture is becoming more fit and athletic inbuilt. We can now easily see others who they truly are aside from their projection of themselves. We can easily view the 3-D reality from the detached calm perspective of merely an unbiased observer. Some of us came here to fight the dark with our light."

Remember that we, the CHADD and me the God Duo, came to guide you. And we are bringing you Oneness.

"Some came here to transmute the dark into the light. Some came just to recognize the dark and the light and stand in balance. There is no right or wrong nor right or wrong path. All are just experiences we chose to have in this time-space reality.

Whatever it is...Know that you are doing what you came here for. Never doubt that.

You are always loved and guided, and You are not alone, again we are on this journey together. Just have to learn and have fun with it.

You are now reading this text for an important reason. You are finally ready to receive the truth of your sovereign divinity and to cast off the deliberate forgetting and hiding of your true nature.

It is challenging, but it is a great honor for any soul to be here at this point in time. Just follow your heart. The Earth has made it through the Gateway to the new Universe... our new tomorrow. The Earth is moving into the New Golden Age and it is the Great Awakening. You have much to look forward to in the future on the New Earth. You will find the fountain of youth.

Part of living in higher consciousness is learning to LOVE... Allow... Adjust... and Adapt in Gentle Ways. The new technologies will have opportunities for Healing, which could never have been imagined. Communication will become telepathic. It will be a Great Abundance. Purpose and destiny will come from our hearts. Remembering much more of gifts and abilities.

It will be steadfast on mission because the energy in hearts will be strongly directed to work.
Humanity is coming together in oneness. We are here to be a part of this oneness. We have all suffered from separation but as these new energies continue to shift... you will no longer find separation. It will be living in the Light of the New Earth. Living in the ever-changing present moment and being happy.

But beware of the Trumpets and the Judgments in the book "Revelation". At the heart of the seven trumpets in Revelation are the judgments that come with the blowing of each one. Before the blowing of the seventh and final trumpet, there are a series of events that take place.

"The rest of mankind who were not killed by these plagues (Covid-19 ...) still did not repent of the work of their hands; they did not stop worshiping demons, and idols of gold, silver, bronze, stone, and wood—idols that cannot see or hear or walk. Nor did they repent of their murders, their magic arts, sorcery, their sexual immorality or their thefts" (Rev. 9:20-21).

"The seventh angel sounded his trumpet, and there were loud voices in heaven, which said: 'The kingdom of the world has become the kingdom of our Lord and of his Messiah, and he will reign forever and ever" (Revelation 11:15).

So, it is time to take care of you. It is time to pray and meditate. It is the time for repentance. Time to Love one another and make it part of the saved ones."

CHAPTER 3
A Spiritual Battle For Humanity

It's the end of these two thousand years of cycles and the control of humanity. Freedom is within reach. The golden age. But the controllers have a dark agenda.

I have been downloading information from me in another timeline about what is happening now. It is related to history and the past two thousand years. The more I am aware of my thoughts, feelings, and perceptions, The higher my level of consciousness of internal and external events and surroundings.

I was in a high state of consciousness when I entered the scene. It was blurry and I could not figure out where I was at first. It was so sudden I got a bit confused for a few seconds. The connection continues…

"The place where I came from is with wisdom" I heard "I am here to help you. I will come to give it to you automatically. It is given to you from your consciousness, and now I am here to bring you that. I came to share my wisdom. Listen carefully, There can be peace at the end. But you must know, that freedom that is at peace must be earned.

The cabal has set up a dark agenda. The controllers, the self-elected elite in key places, freedom for you is not in their plan they do not want to end their control on humans. Will the population be able to open their eyes, and start to expand their awareness to see through, It depends. Because there is violence and fake news spread to distract. It is outrageous that they are misleading human beings, but it is part of their agenda. People need to wake up and break free! Or they will be left out.

There is invasion in countries and destruction with the help of their leaders. There is a fanatical political organization that uses fear to reality and facilitates people's thinking that somehow they are the saviors. But really what people are doing is helping them accomplish their goal. It is a global public-private fascist movement and fusion of big Government, big tech, and big money to create a technocratic ruling elite, which conveniently is them. The oligarchs running the world are pedophiles controlling the global child trafficking systems.

They wanted to create feudalism, in which humans were serfs, and they would be the lords ruling over. And that is what they are aiming for. What it is, is there is a battle out for humanness setting the context for every of these events happening. Every event that is unfolding in the world is a battle for something deep within each of you, so precious that nations will go to war with other nations to keep you distracted.

There is a spiritual battle for humanity, transhumanism, DNA, AI, and the forgotten past. There is a movement to replace the human body with synthetic chemicals and blood sensors. Change of DNA. There are the skin computer chips, in the brain, the mark of the beast. There is Artificial Intelligence and robots. It steals from humans the ability to access this precious part. Humanness is about to give away what it means to be fully human. The essential to give up individual freedoms and turn over rules to experts. This whole agenda is to make it, so people have no choice on some of the biggest questions of their lives. This is happening because at these meetings they meet, and they work together with government and corporate to bypass democracy and impose things through fascist corporate government.

People were indoctrinated and got vaccinated to be able to travel the world, go on vacations, to simply be able to eat in restaurants. While some did not understand fully the consequences of having DNA changed. And unfortunately, many have already died from the vaccinations, with heart attack, blood clots or having developed cancer."

And appeared in a vision pointing to Earth, an Angel with his right hand. The Angel cried out in a loud voice: "Penance, penance, penance! Pray much and make sacrifices for sinners. For many souls go to Hell because there is no one to pray for them" White roses were falling from the sky and Our Lady said "Only some will be cured while the Lord has no confidence in others who were not killed" Blessed Mother Mary revealed herself as the Lady of the Rosary and said: "People must amend their lives, ask forgiveness for their sins and not offend our Lord any more for He is already too much offended."

And Mother Mary offered the Fatima Prayer:
"O my Jesus, forgive our sins, save us from the fires of hell, Lead all souls to Heaven, especially those most in need of Thy mercy. Amen." When the Earth changes over, then benevolent hybrids and ET species will then be sent all around the Earth to sort of be guides and help everyone with the change. Every moment you hesitate, the clock ticks closer to the hour when silence equates to surrender. It is Time.

A good protocol to Detox from spike Proteins (given by an angel to help you.) There are 3 key supplements to degrade spike proteins and reduce inflammation. To avoid cardiac arrests and major blood clots.

1. Natto kinase: 2000 units twice a day
2. Bromelain: 500 milligrams once a day (Both degrade the spike protein in different ways.)
3. Curcumin: 500 milligrams twice a day (to reduce inflammation and spike protein damage)

CHAPTER 4
Prophetic Knots and the Puzzle

It was in April, clear and blue sky, a shining sun, just a light and comfortable breeze blowing. I was sitting on my patio enjoying the perfect weather, and now I am being pulled up. I am floating and I see a bright light.

The next thing I know is that I am entering an amazing place. Everything seems to be filled with light. There is a fountain in the middle and stream water is falling on crystals. All sorts of crystals with very colorful birds singing. A man with white hair greets me. The place is like a library. People come here to research. The man takes me to another room. The room is different but also very nice. There is one wall that is just a solid window with light and there are shelves and rows of books. In the center of the room, there is a table, and the man takes me to this table. There is a chair for me, and I sit on it. The man looked at me and said," You know what to do next" I replied I wasn't sure. "He said, "You do know… now call the book at you." When I opened the book I read: "Any doubts or worries you have been having are going to be finally resolved and you are going to feel a whole weight lifted off your shoulders. You asked if you had to ask to receive. The answer was there, it was there no need to ask for that. The father will do it."

It reminded me that I was always referring to obstacles in my destiny as knots. But I also remember

Mother Mary undoing it. It happened when I was at the location of the three Marys in France. They were put by Katherine (the surrogate) and Paul when Katherine twisted and bent my reality, and I knew it, said the Gallican Catholic Priest. But no one believed me or understood it. So, I called these obstacles Knots and always referred to my reality, linked to my future destiny with my blue flame, as a puzzle with all the pieces that needed to fall and to fit into places.

Still, in my chair looking at the book, there was a merging of my thoughts and my vision. It was very weird. When I heard the phone ringing, I tried to go back to my dream vision. But the vision involved a short, beautiful woman with a tiny diamond in her nose. She was the same short height as the one I saw during a three-day convention that had a metallic voice. I was seized by this absolute sense of picking up the phone to hear it. I had to hear it. I had to know who it was, and who was disturbing my vision, and at the same time it was part of it. So, I picked up the call and it was CHADD, he needed to tell me about his dream, and a woman with a tiny diamond in her nose. "It's important that you know who she is," he said. She is the voodoo woman, and I am unlocking some knots that she did in our lives and now the puzzle is slowly falling into place. It's a piece of positive information"

"Does it make sense to you?" He asked me. Yes, I replied to total sense. It's a confirmation of Mother Mary's undoer of knots. I have asked her to help. She is probably undoing it through you as you are part of it. The voodoo woman used you while she kept you on drugs in the back of her house with the system. These short times when she was not putting you in some State mental hospitals while she was enjoying the money she was paid for putting you there. They were experimenting and using you and your brain, and she was paid as your guardian. And now all is coming into place, and it will be known. And Paul also will be uncovered. We are both finally going to be free. It has already arrived in another realm.

The following night, Ambassador Asuba appeared to me and confirmed "Now I have full power, and I am helping you. I heard your request. I liberate you and help you have more freedom." Wow! Thank you.

That's the same night when CHADD heard 23 knocks on his bedroom's wall twice and commanded the spirit to go. He knew I was writing about this numerological number and informed me right away. And I knew this was important information because it was bothering the dark energies. Then I saw the message "No one escapes the Universe's judgement.

CHAPTER 5

Cutting The Restrictions With Golden Scissors

On that day I was up earlier than usual and fixing my breakfast when I saw, through the window, a green cloud in the sky. The cloud light was beautiful, and it grew and grew as more and more people around the world sent me love and blessings. It grew then they saw me as a spirit, lifting around the sky.

I quickly called Saint Michael the Archangel into the battle for my protection and my defense and spoke "O St Michael Prince of the heavenly host by the Divine Power of God, be our defense in the battle against the wickedness and the snares of the devil. May God rebuke him, I humbly pray and thrust into the pit of hell Satan and his minions, all the evil and dark spirits who prowl around the world seeking to ruin souls and destroy humanity."

That's when Wanda Harmon, from the Soul Advisory Council Unification of the Lightworker, appears. She saw all that was done to me and came to cut with golden scissors the restrictions I had on me for years.

As helpers and protectors, I am now sent to connect with three spiritual animals the Gecko (from New Caledonia Island), a Peacock, and a Butterfly. My left underarm pit is under attack and has a horrible and painful blister that has been put purposely on my feminine side. This painful pimple is located on my female side to stop me from my Goddess energy. And I see that these attacks have lasted for years.

After Wanda came to my help it's now another beautiful person that appears. "I am Elyse Pakaro," she said. I am a Harmonic Doctor born and raised in Greece into a family of gifted healing psychics, and I have inherited the gift." Elyse Pakaro has now left the physical world and come to my help. She is flooding my body with yellow which is a healing and intelligent connection and surrounding it with pink. Elyse is now in the other realm a spiritual Lightworker physician and she came to help me. This attack is trying to stop me, and it also closes my throat which is inflamed now by the attack.

After my mission work, I was sent overseas for nineteen months I had to fly back to continue my mission with my blue flame, and I had to take the three times within a week the Covid-19 test. When they forced me to take the COVID-19 test again upon arrival at the destination some dark energy took the opportunity to destroy my membrane's protection in my nose. It's some tiny hairs called cilia that help to filter the air and dark energy took also the occasion to infect me with a virus connected to the skin in my nose.

These cilia are tiny, hair-like structures that are free-floating in the nose and sinus cavity. When they are healthy, they beat 14-16 times per second. Clippers and tweezers have no effect on these hairs, but they can be paralyzed or even killed off by diesel fumes, cigarette smoke, and other pollutants. Nasal hair is different from the cilia of the ciliated lining of the nasal cavity. And now Elyse has come to my help because I am lacking some yellow.

It is when my spiritual guides decided to call the Priest Father Damien who used to work with Lepers in Hawaii on a Catholic mission to work with my skin. Father Damien, unfortunately, caught leprosy and died from it.

Now, it is the turn of my guide Ambassador Asuba. He liberates me so that I'll have more freedom, and he takes away the cataract and the closing of my third eye. Thank God! And Ambassador Asuba I have been working blind for so long.

I am told that now my most important mission is to form a spiritual group. I am asked by my guides to keep forming a spiritual group of people and get as many as I can. More than in other times it is necessary that the Lightworkers come together. To be part of the group they will have some specific restrictions. No Ego, No judging, and No money must be involved. Pure loving and friendly souls only.

The Ambassador explained that covid vaccinations contain microbes and AI in vaccinations and they are programmed to change the DNA and there is an agenda behind it. The Global politic of vaccination is accelerating and making worse the Covid and it weakened your immune system. This vaccination is to install a world civilization dehumanized. Once vaccinated if you catch it you have more chance to die from it. It does not help to eliminate it but to spread it wider. It creates a pandemic.

I am made aware of what happened with my crippled hands. A ceremony was made to my hands by the Gallican Catholic Exorcist Priest who is also a Knight Templar. This was to transform a ritual that was done to stop my hands from moving by the nut islander's girl who contacted a crazy person in France to do so. The poor girl burned her neurons using drugs for years.

CHADD's body went through so much that I became seriously worried. Plus, I could not do much for him as I was myself without transportation and a house. I had, like him to live with relatives.

That is when a high Light Arcturian heard my concern about CHADD health. His body has gone through so many attacks, poisons, drugs, surgeries, and battles I was reflecting on requesting to have him lifted on board an Arcturians spaceship and to be put in a member to repair his body and have his organs regrow so that he will not ever go back under an earth surgeon care anymore. The high Light Arcturian person decided to make it the following night.

And that is exactly when my ancestor Elesteau, my ancestor that is my guide, and with me now decided to come and help. He appeared to help previously a few years ago once under the name of Pierre Montour de la Roue, and today he came under the name of Elesteau. It must be that he is in another life or another timeline. He is the one who received the chevron and passed it to me.

So, my ancestor Elesteau is now a healer's guide. He is working on me and will work on CHADD also. CHADD will have a complete body, auric, and chakra scan. While doing it he found some damage and CHADD was in need of turquoise and blue Color harmonic frequency infusion for his healing.

As I needed and was in lack of yellow infused in my body, and some pink surrounding my body. In my etheric body. I will also be transported in the spaceship during my sleep, the same night that CHADD he said. And I would go under Holographic ring, alignment, and re-establish a new normal. When I re-entry into the earth, when I came back my left side was affected. And now it will be much stronger resistance after. So, I asked for help with my body and my health. For regeneration and rejuvenation and for a complete re-balance at the same time so that we will recover both and catch up physically.

Suddenly I could hear many voices speaking at the same time. And I received long messages that flashed into my head, and it was about the number twenty-three connected to restoring balance, and to human sex cells containing one complete set of twenty-three chromosomes.

"When the Awakened Masculine meets the true, Feminine, it arouses a new sensation in him and activates specific levels of consciousness that demand his full attention.

The Awakened, Whole, Consciousness Feminine does not act needy or desperate around the Masculine. This does not mean that she does not acknowledge her deep inner desire and sacred requirements for the Masculine presence to be in her life. She knows this better than any woman who has not yet opened to her full powers and strengths

The awakened woman knows that the Masculine plays a vital role in her life journey and can open her up in ways that she cannot do alone. In essence, she wants the Masculine from a searingly profound place in her Soul. But this 'want' can be put on hold for years and years, decades even if she is not being met with the kind of Masculine presence and devotion that she needs to serve her sacred Feminine role.

When the Masculine meets the conscious Feminine vibration, it instantly realizes what is needed. The Masculine energy is stirred deeply and feels a pull on the Soul strings of his lost, dry, and forgotten heart. He realizes that although it is easy to lose himself in the glorious female principle of divine energy, and power sway of her body, and the warmth of her sacred eyes, to stand next to her as a totem of Divine Masculine strength he must rise in his own life. Her spiritual energy will cause his own to wake up to itself.

He will become quickly aware that it will not be enough to lazily get what he wants and leave. He will recognize that even if he enters a relationship with her, her trust in him will not deepen unless he starts seriously showing up in his own life and begins to rise like a phoenix toward his Full Purpose. Her awakened energy will not tolerate the spiritually sleepy Masculine tendencies towards laziness, denial, avoidance, staying in comfort zones, procrastination, cowardice, and over-reliance on quick fixes and instant gratification.

Her sacred energy will pull him up out of his coma and avoidance tactics, so that he feels on a visceral level just how potent and transformational loving her could be. He will also feel how loving her – and being a recipient of the healing codes in her body – instigates a firing of the neurons and electrical transmitters in his system, sparking him into awareness of just how much of a man he is required to evolve into.

He realizes that she is the greatest gift that has ever crossed his path. He realizes that he may never have another opportunity like this one to be supported in becoming the best version of himself possible. He is aware that there is no other woman on the planet who could love him like this and fire up his energy centers into creating the Divine Purpose he has always wanted to live but has always been too scared to fully commit to.

It is his decision whether he is brave enough to take the challenge of loving, and standing next to, a woman who has claimed her place as a sacred Feminine warrior and the holy chalice of love.

It is his decision in many ways, because although she will be the one to decide whether she wishes to see him again or let him into her world – she is always doing that based on the quality of truth, assurance, purposefulness, and willingness that she receives from him.

When his Higher Self brings him to a Whole Woman, he must sit and contemplate, to realize that he has chosen this meeting, because a significant part of him is ready to ascend into being a Whole Man. This is a huge deal because he most likely has not had any role models of this evolved male energy in his life. He doesn't have to be faultless, a know-it-all, flashy, or a good-looking movie star good-looking. He only must nurture that spark within his precious Masculine heart that wants to be the best man he can be. He only must be willing and humble enough to learn from the Feminine, listen to her responses to his actions, and realize that she is the Divine Oracle for him, showing him where he needs to pull himself up.

His Soul only wants to bathe in the sweet, sacred radiance of your eternal Light for the rest of its days and remember daily what a gift you are to its Soul. Wanting you to be the Sacred Mirror in all the ways that he sabotages itself, denies itself, restricts itself, and 'flunks out' on itself.

He wants to hear that you trust him and wants to show you that your trust is well-judged and that he realizes how your ability to trust him makes a difference in how deeply you can open your body and heart when you are together.

He wants to walk into brave new territories, risking rejection and even failure so that your trust in him soars, like a bird in flight. Realizing that your sexual attraction to him increases exponentially every time he takes a risk to rise into his Divine Masculine power and purpose.

He wants to be a pioneer of a new movement of conscious, evolving, willing and open-hearted males, defying the old paradigms and awake enough to walk beside women who are changing the world forever.

He might not remember any of this, much of the time, and he may stumble, fall, collapse, or sometimes fail at it. He wants only to remember that his willingness to live its Sacred Truth, and his desire to do everything he can to earn your trust, are enough. He wants only to remember that if he shuts down his heart at the first hint of truth that comes from his mouth, his body language, and his expressions, he will not win this game. He wants to only remember that you cannot be expected to 'mother' him into being a grown-up (if he wants to have a sexually vital and transformative love life). He does not want you to be his mother.

We need manifestos for men of the Light to follow now because they must stand up and realize their true worth and value in the advancing New Age. Awake Women do not want to batter men, criticize them, punish them, or shut their hearts and bodies down to them. Whole Women want men: their unwavering hard presence, their rock-solid actions, their warrior hearts, their dynamic, pursuing energy.

Many Men of the Light are choosing to cross paths with soul-embodied women now. This is because their Soul recognizes that it is time to rise into Purpose, and the desire to connect with the embodied Sacred Feminine will ignite that Purpose. A woman who is on the path of Light will not settle for any man, no matter how deeply she has longed for the masculine presence. She has no desire nor energy to rescue, mother, nag or coach a man into loving her.

Yet the awakened woman carries more compassion, more unconditional love, more ability to support and nurture, more generosity, and more sexual power than any other. There are limitless, never-ending, eternally abundant rewards for any man who is courageous enough to risk his heart and life purpose for such a female.

This is the time of the emergent Divine Masculine presence, stepping up to the edge and committing to live from there, rising up to support and protect the Sacred Feminine Mission of Global Awakening." And the voices stopped.

CHAPTER 6
CHADD and VIE Reunion Guided By The Father

A few weeks later the visions of the future continue. I understand that people who cannot or will not accept the ideas of the new era fall ill spiritually. They do not find their place among people and fall into deep spiritual conflict. The great initiator leads his people up to the threshold of the new epoch, up to the borders of the promised land. The chosen ones who are called to proclaim and carry out the new epoch wander onward, guarding the wisdom and the secret teaching.

Guided by the father the God Duo meets again. CHADD arrived first and went for a coffee. Entering the place where he met VIE on May 8. He immediately saw that the place was full of generals. CHADD went straight to the counter to ask for a coffee, and at the time of paying that's where he recognized the voice of the motorcycle saying, "Leave it it's mine" He immediately recalled what happened three days earlier and knew that was God's will. He was offered three packs of flower seeds to plant.

As they barely finished eating lunch a text arrived on VIE's phone. She pulled it out of her purse and read. "I am in bed. My stomach is very upset. I did not eat anything. Can you come to help? She went to a friend's house with the kids and left me alone" Really! VIE thoughts.

"Very upset by the text she read. She knew what she read was true, and that he was the tool to an evil work. Once again it was an attempt by an evil spirit to keep the two isolated and separated. Of course, she took all her time knowing that it was a ruse again.

CHADD entered a trance and received messages from the father for VIE. The first message was about wearing a mask "I have given you a mouth, use it, he said" Why would you cover it? Think about it. Since (COVID-19) people on Earth must wear a mask. Like they have been given an immune system to battle the disease.

The second message was about the family and a personal message for VIE from the father through CHADD's voice "Jesus, Marie, and Joseph." Then VIE was instructed to read in the bible Job and Jeremiah. "Then the word of the Lord came to me, saying. Before I formed thee in the belly I knew thee, and before thou calmest forth out of the womb I sanctified thee, and I ordained thee a prophet unto the nations. Then said I, Ah, Lord God! Behold I cannot speak; for I am a child.

But the Lord said unto me, Say not, I am a child: for though shalt go to all I shall send there, and whatsoever I command thee thou shalt speak. Be not afraid of their faces: for I am with thee to *deliver* thee, saith the Lord. Then the Lord put forth his hand and touched my mouth. And the Lord said to me, Behold, I have put my words in thy mouth.

See, I have this day set thee over the nations and the kingdoms, to root out, and to pull down, and to destroy, and to throw down, to build, and to plant." Jeremiah chapter 1:4-10.

"Then the Lord said unto me…Out of the North an evil shall break forth upon all the inhabitants of the Land. For I will call all the families of the kingdoms of the north, said the Lord; and they shall come, and they shall set everyone his throne at the entering of the gates of Jerusalem, and against all the walls thereof round about, and against all the cities of Judah."

"Moreover, the word of the Lord came unto me, saying, Je-re-mi'ah, what sees though? And I said I see a rod of an almond tree. Then said the Lord unto me. Thou hast well seen for I will hasten my word to perform it. And the word of the Lord came into me the second time, saying, What sees you? And I said I see a seething pot: and the face thereof is towards the north. Then the Lord said to me. Out of the north, an evil shall break forth upon all inhabitants of the land.

For, lo, I will call all the families of the kingdoms of the north, saith the Lord; and they shall come. And they shall set everyone his throne at the entrance of the gates of Jerusalem and against all the walls thereof round about, and all the cities of Judah.

And I will utter my judgments against them touching all their wickedness, who have forsaken me, and have burned incense unto other gods, and worshipped the works of their own hands. Thou, therefore, gird up thy loins and arise, and speak unto them all that I command thee: be not dismayed at their faces, lest I confound thee before them.

For, Behold, I have made thee this day a defenced city, and an iron pillar, and braised walls against the whole land, against the Kings of Judah, against the princes thereof, against the priests thereof, and the people of the land.

And they shall fight against thee, but they shall not prevail against thee; for I am thee, saith the Lord, to deliver thee. Jeremiah 1:11-19.

"Moreover, the word of the Lord… came to me saying, Go and cry in the ears of Jerusalem, saying. Thus, saith the Lord; I remember thee, the kindness of thy youth, the love of thine espousals, when thou wentest after me in the wilderness, in a land that was not sown. Jeremiah 2:1-2

CHAPTER 7

The Seven – A Magical Number

There was no sound but a fresh smell. I traveled through Galaxies and stars moving at an incredible speed. I felt an incredible sense of peace. Joy and oneness. A man started talking, and the man was looking for conversing with someone or something above him. At that moment my consciousness was as clear as in the daytime. He was talking to me.

You are electrical, and our atoms are surrounded by electrons (electricity). We are connected to the earth's electromagnetic fields and our heart is our battery. Many of your ancient spiritual figures knew this hidden knowledge and meditated or prayed on these lines or megalithic centers, which elevated their electrical auras, intellect, and connection to higher self, through the activation of the 7 energy centers (chakras, which are vortexes of energy centers.)

In the human body, you have the 7 chakras which are energetically interdependent and activated sequentially. Similarly in this model, the Earth has a chakra system, arranged not anatomically but in energy sequence at 7 key Dome centers.

It is scientifically verified that 7 is when the universe is connected with you.

777 means synchronicity is happening to you. Universal is the source of energy to communicate with

you. There are 7 Divisions on the Physical Plane and the Rainbow has 7 Colors, the Energy known as Sound has 7 notes in Music and the same note recurs on the eighth key, only it has a higher or lower Pitch according to which side of the Scale is reckoned. Each complete Scale of Notes is called Septave or "Saptaka" meaning the series of the seven notes. The Scale of Seven. Seven the anti-New World Order.

There are seven Catholic Sacraments:

1- The Sacrament of Baptism
2- The Sacrament of Confirmation
3- The Sacrament of Holy Communion
4- The Sacrament of Penance (Confession)
5- The Sacrament of Mariage
6- The Sacrament of Holy Orders
7- The Sacrament of Anointing the Sick.

0010110 is the sign of the 7th stars of the Pleiades

- 7 Sacraments
- 7 Spirits in Front of the thrown
- 7 Layers of Heaven
- 7 Tiers of Crown

Number seven is mostly connected to the stars of Pleiades in the sky where angels of Light in the scripture come from. The Pleiades and the Galactic Federation are the Elohim of mankind.

Jesus said that the "Son of Man" (like humans) "would fill the Heavens" (UFOs), immediately before we "change in the blink of an eye" Which is the ascension, and "take us to a place prepared for us to a dwelling" which is density and dimensions."

John's vision of the last days describes a supernatural, white-haired creator (Pleiadian), holding a symbol of the 7 Stars. (The Pleiades)

- 7 Stars
- 7 Lanterns
- 7 Angels
- 7 Trumpets
- 7 Temples
- 7 The Seven Sisters

Holy Orders is the sacrament by which bishops, priests and deacons are ordained and receive the power and grace to perform their sacred duties. The sacred rite by which orders are conferred is called ordination. The apostles were ordained by Jesus at the Last Supper so that others could share in his priesthood.

The Babylonians divided their lunar months into 7 days and weeks, with the final day of the week holding particular religious significance. The twenty-eight days month, or a complete cycle of the Moon, was a bit too large a period of time to manage effectively, and so the Babylonians divided their month into four equal parts of 7.

There are 7 days in a week and 7 Planets.

Seven seems to be a magical number in many cultures and is often imbued with mystical and religious attributes. In the Abrahamic faiths, for instance, it is believed that God created the world in seven days, while in Greek mythology, the Pleiades were seven sisters who were the companions of the goddess Artemis.

Healing Powers of the Seventh Son of a Seventh Son, in European folklore, the 7th son of a 7th son is believed to possess special powers. Such a child is said to be gifted with the power to heal diseases.

The "seven deadly sins" were originally based on a list of eight principal vices. In the sixth century, Pope Gregory I changed Cassian's list of eight vices into the list of seven deadly, or cardinal, sins of Roman Catholic theology: pride, greed, lust, envy, gluttony, anger, and sloth. Gregory viewed these as capital, or principal, sins in that many other sins came from them.

And 7.5 Hz is the frequency of the Earth used by the wise Masters to sit under a tree and meditate. It is a brain wave associated with rest, relaxation, and meditation in ancient times.

"If you want to find the Key to the universe, think in terms of energy, frequency and vibration - Nikola Tesla -"

The 7 Energetics Centers or 7 Musical Notes
The Power of Music and the frequency of 432 HZ

"Music is a moral law. It gives a soul to the Universe, wings to the mind, flight to the imagination, a charm to sadness, gaiety and life to everything. It is the essence of order and leads to all that is good and just and beautiful. "Plato Music can control. You can kill with it; it can keep you in a vegetative state or be Florissant depending on the type of music. Rests have been done on animals and plants.

You have seven energetics centers, linked to seven notes, Do, Re, Me, Fa, Sol, La, Si. All these notes correspond to an organ, and each organ corresponds to a color, and each corresponds to its frequency.

But what you do not know is that each amino acid has also its frequency. And you have the "Canon of Pachelbel 432 HZ". This is something I advise you to listen to every day. It is the only music that nourishes you and the essential amino acid. It contains eight tones which correspond to eight essential amino acids. It has been created in such a way that even if you start listening in the middle of it, it is like you started to listen to it at the beginning. It regulates your metabolism, and it is a powerful anti-stress. It activates your enzymatic systems and your protein.

If we had a world bathing in 432 HZ, we would be more joyful, more alive and we would be much more intuitive.

CHAPTER 8

The Healing Power of the Gregorian Chants; The 7 tone of sequence of....

The day has finally arrived. I have been preparing for this journey for a long time. After a two-hour drive, I am finally entering the Benedictine Monastery Church. It smells Holy and Sacred. There is a mix of scents of the old wood benches with the Monks' Energies in prayers inside the building. One can feel the Divine presence that brings respect, harmony, and joy to my heart.

In the far front of the Monastery, the Monks are sitting in silent prayers. I enjoy looking at their glowing faces.

One of the Monk sees me and now comes towards me with a jovial face. He welcomes me:

"Welcome, please come in, I was waiting for you. It is perfect timing we will begin soon to chant. we are aware of what is happening to CHADD, and we know that he cannot meet us today, but he is the one who sent you here today. He told us that he still will be present in mind"

I receive information from the Monk regarding the spectrum of Sound, the solfeggio frequencies, and the Gregorian Chants.

The Benedictine Monks explains that as we are moving into a new process of Love environment and pain remitted, where new experiences come through.

Spirituality becomes above the manipulated duality world and mankind discovers their purpose in life. It is perfect timing; he says we will begin soon to chant. But let me explain.

Solfeggio frequencies are from an ancient scale that was said to be rediscovered by Dr. Joseph Puleo. Solfeggio frequencies were lost for many years, and it was re-introduced in 1100 CE, by the Catholic Church.

The Gregorian Chants and their special tones were believed to impart spiritual blessings when sung in harmony. Each Solfeggio tone is comprised of a frequency required to balance your energy and keep your body, mind, and spirit in perfect harmony. It is quite impressive the value that ancient civilizations would give to the power of music. Ancient civilizations from all areas of the world seemed to use music as therapy, in all of its forms. The Greeks used flutes or lyres, the Mesopotamians used the harp, and the Incas used the flutes (quena).

They are a 7-tone sequence of special electromagnetic frequencies originally used in Gregorian chants many hundreds of years ago, and recently, they were brought back to everybody's attention for their healing powers. These frequencies induce movements of consciousness that will help stimulate new changes that are necessary for individuals who would like to achieve awakening. They were used in over 150 Gregorian chants.

Each syllable was thoroughly studied by Dr. Puleo and other professional researchers. David Hulse, a sound therapy pioneer with over 40 years of experience, described the tones as the following:

★ UT - 396 Hertz: DO, color red. Turning grief into joy, Liberating Guilt and fear, and how they can suppress other emotions as well.

★ 417 Hertz: RE. Color orange. Undoing situations and facilitating change. It is related to past trauma and negativity and the willingness to change. This frequency can help you to recognize past traumas that are no longer valuable in your life.

★ MI 528 Hertz: MI, color yellow Transformation & miracles, repair DNA. Peace of mind and clarity. This frequency will help you heal and remove any sickness you may have.

★ 639 Hertz: FA, color Green. Connecting with spiritual family. It is related to Interpersonal relationships and this frequency.

★ 741 Hertz: SOL, color blue. Expression and solution. It is related to the emotional stability you are looking for. Cleaning and solving.

★ 852 Hertz: LA, color indigo. Returning to Spiritual Order. It is related to the views of oneself and the universe.

★ 963 Hertz: SI, purple is usually related to the feeling of oneness. It means awakening and being interconnected to the universe. This frequency helps you to reconnect with yourself. It is associated with purple.

7 Energetics Centers or 7 Musical Notes

"Music is a moral law. It gives a soul to the Universe, wings to the mind, flight to the imagination, a charm for sadness, gaiety, and life to everything. It is the essence of order and leads to all that is good and just and beautiful". -Plato

The Power of Music and the Frequency of 432 HZ. Music can control you. You can kill with it; it can keep you in a vegetative state or be Florissant depending on the type of music. Tests have been done on animals and plants.

You have seven energetics centers, linked to seven notes, Do, Re, Me, Fa, Sol, La, Si. All these notes correspond to an organ, and each organ corresponds to a color, and each corresponds to its frequency.

But what you do not know is that each amino acid has also its frequency. And you have the "canon of Pachelbel 432 HZ". This is something I advise you to listen to every day. It is the only music that nourishes you and the essential amino acid. It contains eight tones which correspond to eight essential amino acids. It was created in such a way that even if you start listening in the middle of it, it is like you started to listen to it at the beginning. It regulates your metabolism, and it is a powerful anti-stress. It activates your enzymatic systems and your protein.

If we had a world bathing in 432 HZ, we would be more joyful, more alive and we would be much more intuitive.

Popular legend credits Pope Gregory I with inventing the Gregorian chants, and scholars believe that it arose from a later synthesis of Roman chant and Gallican Catholicism.

Gregorian chant developed mainly in Western and Central Europe during the 9th and 10th centuries. Rhythm is very important to Gregorian chant. This is the Solesmes method.

The Gregorian chant also called the chant of the Franks is the style that eventually propagated to the whole Catholic world.

After Vatican II, the use of the Gregory chant declined rapidly within the Catholic Church. One cause of the decline was the change in the language of the Catholic Church services, from Latin, which is the language of the Gregorian chant to the "vernacular" which is the language of each country.

The Gregorian chant has been present in the world much before Jesus Christ or even Pope Gregory the First, for that matter on the face of the Earth.

Church leaders at St. John the Beloved made the bold decision in 2005 to switch its music from the praise and worship genre to sacred music featuring Gregorian chant, decades after the practice fell out of favor following the Second Vatican Council.

The ancient traditional Gregorian chant MUST, therefore, in a large measure be restored to the functions of public worship. Special efforts are to be made to restore the use of the Gregorian chant by people, so that the faithful may again take a more active part in the ecclesiastical offices, as was the case in ancient times.

This 7-tone sequence of special electromagnetic frequencies has been blocked on purpose by dark energies. The number seven is the anti-New World Order

To get the best from the Solfeggio Frequencies listen to it for 14-28 days for a minimum of 10 minutes to reap the benefits. Sitting, on your couch, on the floor, or laying down, or on the floor, doing activities, working, relaxing, sleep. Whatever resonates the best with you. Listen for 14 - 28 days for noticeable results and a positive shift. Many experience a shift happening after the first couple of seconds of listening, some take longer.

I could no longer see the visions.

CHAPTER 9
An Important Number Twenty-Three

I keep hearing this in my head again and again in my sleep:

"Even though I walk through the darkest valley, I will fear no evil, for you are with me; your rod and your staff, they comfort me".

-Psalm 23

Did you know that women have been chosen by God to be the portal between the spiritual realm and the physical realm? Women are the only force on earth powerful enough to navigate unborn spirits onto this planet.

Spirituality and physicality are inseparable. Our job as the God Duo is not only to help inform humanity, in some cases, as to what is occurring but to stay in peace and hold the light while all is unfolding around you. Our Job is to Hold the Light. Humanity still needs to continue to awaken to what you have endured for millennia. You cannot fix a problem if you do not know what the problem is.

It all begins with one person, one soul, expanding their light from within. Remember the Divine is within you, not outside yourself up in the heavens somewhere. There is no power outside yourself. The source is within you. Your higher aspects of self are not "out there". Remember this!

During my 'sleep,' I felt intense love. I was listening to music in my bed and was asking myself questions about the infinity of the Universe. Suddenly I was welcomed by sublime beings.

"It is finally your time, your turn, your year. The alignment of the stars is not a coincidence, but a God's incident. You have an important soul mission and a higher purpose in life that involves teaching and serving humanity in a way that suits your personality, interests, and natural abilities.

As many have been observing, there is a split happening. This is a free-will planet, every single soul will have the choice to ascend. Every single soul chooses what they want to experience here, and you need to honor that. All will be given a choice.

Have compassion for all. This is everyone's journey, honor their journey, honor the divine within. The matrix is crumbling, this is the change that was wanted by all.

Twenty-three is known as several diplomacies, cooperation, and partnerships, and symbolizes your soul mission and your service to other people.

Twenty-three is associated with your creativity, joy, and imagination. Also, there might be some mystery in this number, but you can be sure that it will symbolize your spiritual growth. If you want to search for a deeper meaning of the number 23, you should also take into account that this number can depend on the number 5 as well, because 2 + 3 gives 5.

It is also known as a number that is related to your health, as well as to your senses and pleasures. This number will motivate you to keep developing your talents and to believe in yourself.

The number 23 derives part of its meaning from the fact that Adam and Eve produced twenty-three daughters according to the first-century historian Josephus (Jewish tradition).

While Eve was equal in value to Adam, God created her with a unique role. It was not good for a man to be alone. So, God decided to create Eve as a helper suitable for him. (Genesis 2:18, 21-24). God also ordained marriage as one flesh union between one man and a woman for life (Matthew 19:3-6.

Psalm 23 is perhaps the most well-known and popular of all the Psalms. King David, who wrote it, sings of God's protection, guidance, refreshment, abundant blessing, and promise of eternal life to those who love him.

The Return of the Goddess is unstoppable and all Starseeds are called to continue the support of the worldwide healing of Planet Terra through resting, through silence, through their own healings as well as through the various planetary healings and meditations.

It has also become a lot safer for the Goddess Energy now to come back to Earth and bring urgently needed healing to torn humanity and Starseeds to prepare them for First Contact. This will happen via Goddess Walk-ins, but more about that in the second part of this Major Planetary Update, which will be about the Return of the Maries/Goddesses.

The descent of the fertility goddess into the Underworld and her triumphant return brings rejuvenated life to the world.

CHAPTER 10
Atlantis & Lemuria Will Rise Again

My phone rang, I picked it up, it was my friend Ingrid. I just had the time to hear her telling me, "Did you receive it?" and she hung up. My phone rang again, and I heard "Gaby is hearing it". And she hung up again. What is that all about, I am thinking. And here is my answer. Now I have got it.

"I am Ashtar. I come at this time to continue to help and guide them to understand the perspective we have. The perspective we want you all to have too.

When we look down and see Earth, We see life here on the planet. But we see it as it should be. Not necessarily as it is now. We see higher consciousness in all the planet, not those lower awareness spotlights.

Atlantis & Lemuria will rise again. Yes, of course, we are aware of the darkness. We are aware of those dark ones who continue to do everything possible to stop the ascension process, and they've done everything they can to contain it. But understand, they can no longer do it.

As you've heard many times, this is a process. It's not a night-night feeling, at least not at this moment.

You can turn it into that with the Solar Flash. The Solar Flash, the big event, will only happen in divine time that recognizes the awareness of this planet that has risen enough to handle this incoming energy. Because if energy happened now, if Solar Flash were to happen now, many across the planet wouldn't survive.

Don't get emotionally involved or stick to what's happening. Because as you've heard many times, it's an illusion. It's part of the three-dimensional illusion. And it's happening now more and more.

More and more people are realizing that it's also an illusion. And those who still haven't noticed think something is wrong, that something is not right. Something must change. And as they become conscious, just like you, they start questioning things just the way you are and have been. And as they now begin to question, masks will fall off. Their brother and sister's distancing will be a thing from the past.

All that is RETURNING.

They've heard Atlantis and Lemuria will re-emerge. But it will re-emerge within each one of you. Because you carry the memories and remains of those long-forgotten civilizations.

What you expect will finally occur. I know now that an extraordinary period will allow you to accomplish in your favor...<u>A DREAM</u>! The one you've hoped for so long...

Yes, a whole new and much better life awaits you."

I saw the blue spacecraft chip Ashmus commanded by Archangel Michael and next to it the Athena managed by the Arcturian.

I saw that there are an infinite number of parallel realities. It means there are infinite numbers of parallel versions of Earth that co-exist.

I saw that one gift that will be given to you during open contact will be a holographic recording of your complete history.

The recording will go back thousands of years, you will be able to see what Atlantis looked like, to see many civilizations that existed on Earth. That you know nothing about.

It will be history that will be appropriate for the present time in which you will exist. The history will reinforce where you are going into the future. The history you need to know, where you have come from, who you are now, and where you are going. It will be an open eyes history to the agreements you all made with all of us to evolve humanity. To reset humanity in the direction of light, love and joy.

It will be something that your children and grandchildren will look back on, as the time of transformation, the rest of humanity. And they will look back upon Earth from the ships they will be riding in and know the entire planet is truly their home.

There will be no thought of the idea of borders. There will be no different cultures, and they will be cherished and validated. And they will thrive. But there will be a mix of many cultures. Humans hybrids, and other extraterrestrials. You will finally as a planet become a true melting part of the galaxy.

CHAPTER 11

Hyperborean Priests spoke to you on behalf of all Agartha inhabitants

"We are indeed in the middle of intense things happening on all levels now, and these are happening in the invisible realms and mostly on an exceedingly high vibrational frequency level.

The great purification by the Sacred Divine Fires is escalating and indeed this is going to go deeply into the very core of the heart and soul.

The beautiful Sacred Fires are descending and are a beautiful Golden-white-platinum color. This is acting like a huge purification network and indeed I saw how the souls who are ready to ascend and who are purified are lifted into the New Earth and thus new existence.

At the same time, I was clearly shown how souls choose not to go through this process because of fear, and because of clinging to the old. More than this, a deep stuck-ness in the lower frequency bands and thus choosing to stay in what they feel is familiar and refusing to let go of pain and suffering.

This purification process will now truly escalate and indeed it will take some time before all is purified, as each soul will be given the free choice, whether they wish to be purified or not, indeed whether they wish to fully stand in the fullness of their highest soul truth and who and what they in truth are and live it in the New Earth.

Every soul will now be challenged to make these choices.

Indeed, it comes to the fact that each soul is solely responsible for their own choices at this time. As the lifting happens, as said before, two will stand next to each other, one will be lifted, and one will choose to remain. No one can piggyback any other soul into the higher state. It is impossible. One can show the way – but one cannot go through the purification process for another soul and nor can one do this for them.

I have never experienced anything like this before, but indeed, once lifted you assume your new light-body and indeed will not wish to ever sink back into the quagmire of the Old Earth and old 3D again. The challenge though here is to maintain that exceedingly high-frequency band and to grow ever higher and higher into the truth of your Soul and its highest Universal Mastery.

Indeed, this is the moment.

Each one will be given the measure that they are ready to receive and are ready to completely let go of the old, in all and every form and way.

The choice is yours.

For indeed with the Fires of Purification, the Power of Divine Love and Wisdom and Light expands, and the sacred Keys and Codes are activated and given as the soul is ready to receive them. These are Divinely activated.

Indeed, the inner earth energies are now fully reactivated and thus the purification now is happening from deep within and without."

So much is happening and in all aspects of life on planet Earth and indeed the New Earth, more than I can even try to put into words, although I am being shown.

DNA data is collected via COVID tests and Test kits as well as masks are contaminated.

And that's the reason for the constant testing and the ban on wearing homemade or designer masks in certain countries.

Nanotechnology-contaminated human bodies would pose an issue when it comes to being taken onto ships of the Light Forces ... and the Cabal knows that. However, the Light Forces have already initiated countermeasures for this.

And as far as the Galactic Superwave is concerned, the following idea is probably part of the Cabal's plan to seal the planet off and sit out the Event.

As one can see, the density of events is increasing further. That is why mass meditation continues to take place, to stabilize things a bit. It is once again important not to let this drive you crazy, staying centered is the key.

Starseeds should also use the time to prepare not only energetically for the liberation, but also physically. The Light Forces recommend detoxifying the body, especially due to all the information that is coming out now regarding not only vaccinations but also masks and test kits.

A healthy, preferably vegan diet with lots of fruits and vegetables is highly recommended, also a parasite cure and/or enemas. A detoxified body will make ascension and first contact much easier.

Hyperborean Priests are speaking to you on behalf of all Agartha representatives. You probably feel that you are at the very threshold of Ascension.

That is why all of us: other planets' inhabitants and civilizations of the parallel worlds on Earth – are trying to give you support both morally and in terms of energy.

Right now, it is essential to join our efforts to help you eventually throw off the yoke of the Dragon reptiles who seized this beautiful planet.

Now when you see them as they are and you learn about their plans for Earth's population enslavement, you eventually understand that there is no going back to the old life under any circumstances.

Well, how can we help you in this complicated situation?

A long time ago we had to experience something like this: our civilization was destroyed by a technogenic alien race that was at a much lower level of spiritual development.

We could not escape the catastrophe only because we did not fully believe in their pernicious plans.

We judged for ourselves, which, as we can see, is the case with many of you now.

It is difficult for you to realize the fact that those at the helm now can systematically and coolly destroy their own people in the direct meaning of the word.

Many of you still believe they act for your sake, moreover, this is the way that the information about "salvation" v@xx!ne is communicated by all the official mass media to you. But this is exactly what they rely on, on your credibility and, of course, fear for one's life.

Everything was running smoothly according to their plan until the Light Forces stepped in both at the subtle and physical level of Earth.

Agartha inhabitants are no exception, we also contribute our feasible share to the rescue of humanity.

And this is what our help is.

We activate pure genes in your physical bodies since they bear a very powerful Divine code capable of increasing your vibrations in a short time.

As you already know, it is Agartha where the golden gene pool of great civilizations once inhabiting Earth is kept.

And each of you ready for Ascension possesses a particle of this gene pool.

You are the pure and ancient souls who came on Earth to participate in the greatest experiment of the Universe – Transition to a new dimension in your physical bodies.

It is you who once were Lemurians, Atlantes, Hyperboreans…

Your souls have absorbed the experience of these great civilizations, as well as many other – extraterrestrial ones while being born on a variety of planets and dimensions.

Many of you came from very high worlds having artificially decreased your vibrations and chosen Service to people at this supreme moment of their Transition period.

So now, we are working with each of you purifying your DNA in terms of energy from all alien deposits keeping only their Divine "core" – the one they initially featured before the intrusion of the Dragon reptiles to your beloved planet, as well as other low vibration civilizations representatives.

This is what our contribution to humanity's revival is.

As you see, the entire force is at your rescue, and we believe that your victory is not far off now.

Feel Unity with your great King, and let it give you strength and wisdom.

Remember that we are always there for you and shroud you in our Love."

CHAPTER 12

The Story of the Wises Druids

What I am about to share with you here is not known and found in history books.

In ancient times European lands were sacred lands.

The human population living there had great respect for nature and was living in perfect harmony with it. And the Celtic people of ancient times were the wisest. The Druids were the Wises and the Guides were the Celtics. They were living in harmony with nature. The Spirits and the beings of nature gave them the knowledge to heal and cure and a piece of knowledge of how to live in harmony with the land.

Druids had secret locations in which they met to work together with nature, especially with stones. They had the knowledge to store memory in stone so that others could read in the future.

A druid was a member of the high-ranking professional class in ancient Celtic cultures. Perhaps best remembered as religious leaders, they were also legal authorities, adjudicators, lore keepers, medical professionals, and political advisors.

The Druids left no written accounts. While they were reported to have been literate, they are believed to have been prevented by doctrine from recording their knowledge in written form.

The Druids were said to believe that the soul was immortal and passed at death from one person to another. Roman writers also stated that the Druids offered human sacrifices for those who were gravely sick or in danger of death in battle.

Their chief god was the same worshipped by the Phoenicians, the god of the sun. The Druids, like the Celts who came after them, were also very conscious of the dual nature of things. As night follows day, and death follows life, so did all things in life possess their "negative" side.

These sacred mysteries were the same amongst the priests of the Maya...the Druids, and the priests of Egypt, and the same as we practice

CHAPTER 13

Here is how the Creation of Physicians Universities Degree was created

I met Annie one day and I felt guided to go to "Cafe La Baguette" place. I was waiting online for my name to be called and pick up my order when I heard her saying: We are a group of women sitting at the terrace, you belong to this group come with me. I recognized you when I saw your bracelets.

It is winter and it is cold and humid outside, but I am comfortable and warm in bed. I am slowly waking up. My eyes were still closed when a brilliant white light appeared in my sight. I did not want the white light to disappear too quickly. I needed to know why and what it meant. It became even more brilliant, and the light became larger. The white Light was guiding me to write the following. At first, I thought that it was for my friend Annie, as she asked me the previous day "What do you know, asked Annie in a text, about the immune disease system?" But it was more than that.

So, to answer her question I first explained to Annie how the Physicians Universities degrees were created.

The problem that drugstore companies have is that they can't turn energy medicine into pills, trademark, or patent it. They can't sell it, and they are terrified of energy medicines. So, they hide the power behind energy medicine in medical schools. So, what is behind the suppressed awareness of the energy healing power to the public and in medical schools, it is simply because if you are aware of it you cannot benefit from it. They can't make money.

Energy healing is much more effective than chemical healing, the drugs, and pills, and without any side effects.

During the medieval time, the medieval church disagreed that wise women were doing God's healing world. They created universities, professionalizing medicine to be practiced by book-learned men, to wipe out the competition.

And the wise women who practiced God's healing work were natural targets. Unlike university-trained professional physicians, God's gifted women practitioners could offer both knowledge and experience. Little was known about the science behind why their healing worked or didn't, it's understandable that there was believed to be a supernatural element to healing that helped women to be successful healers.

And I continued by saying: but you have to be aware that today, unfortunately, there exist two types of healers. Some are very pro, and some are fear-based, which creates confusion. Fear is a spirit that brings division. However, it is known among spiritual people that these fear-based practitioners will be left in the dust at some point, and they cannot call themselves holistic and natural therapists. If they are for some toxic things and promote putting such a thing in the body. It is separating the real one doing God's work from the people giving voice to it thinking that it's an easy way to make and gain money with.

Then the following Saturday Annie insisted on me visiting a small hidden garden with her. I parked and waited for Annie to come and park. All I saw from my car were people coming back to their cars with plants they bought. It did not make much sense at that time for me. I got out of my car and began to walk towards the park entrance. I still could not make much more sense of this invitation to come here. Why was I here? I started to walk the trail, and it was more about plants than flowers. That's where I was in my thoughts when Annie joined me. I was getting my left eye blind, and it was difficult to walk in the woods. Annie took my hand and asked me to help her walk. She was in pain she said.

Annie met some of her neighbors and began to speak with them. I saw a white rocking share next to a well and decided to go and seat on it. About five minutes later Annie called, she was looking for me. Then she left to enter the old white house behind me.

About ten minutes later she came back. She wanted to introduce me to her friend who will leave soon. She is very intuitive Annie said, she is Hum! Like a gypsy fortune teller. It made not much sense again to me.

The Gypsy woman was introducing some natural kind of juice, had a wellness center, and was traveling invited by corporations, again she said.

CHADD's attitude has changed a lot lately. He was calling me saying that he was confused. Sometimes in the shower did not know how to wash himself, another time he did not understand why he was out of the shower sitting naked when he came back out of the confusion. Most of the time since these episodes of confusion began staying home unable to drive because of confusion and having to watch TV.

I asked him to listen more to music than look at TV, but suddenly he did not have a choice the audio in his bedroom stopped working, like his car speakers stopped working. He had to stay home and watch the TV all day seated next to the archon surrogate, and the two other archons in the house, Paul the surrogate archon and Paul's son the ex-marine archon grand-kid.

I was worried, of course, noticing something that preoccupied me a lot, Katerine the surrogate archon was not reacting to it. These archons working for the elite in control are very sneaky and untrusty. That was her way after three to four weeks of sucking his energy to exhaustion, manipulating his brain to confusion with Paul's help to guide him to ask for a psychotropic drugs prescription again and to make him labeled of autism and ADD.

Coming back home CHADD went to research the side effects of each prescription and found out that one of them was to chemically castrate him. Get him infertile. The same one but generic that the Al Kadir tried to make him infertile years ago. Another one that made its heartbeat and was reducing the blood flow so fast that he had a heart attack etc…

They are slowly reducing the human population to infertility, and we see a rise in the transgender population.

That is when suddenly, CHADD called me and said:

"I went to see the Psychiatrist doctor, Katerine made the appointment for me, I quit all natural supplements, it's dangerous. Like this natural blood pressure, I was taking. My brother told me, there is a very dangerous Japanese flower in it. All these supplements are making me exhausted and confused. And the psychiatrist told me that you are toxic so I should not see you again. Tomorrow I will bring a beautiful ring with many rubies so you will remember me. It is a farewell ring."

Hearing this I began to laugh and laugh, which brought him to silence, and also made him come back to himself. Two days later he said you got me out of my cloudy mind. Thank you. They are trying to kill me with these prescription drugs again.

I sat for a moment in silence and mentally said: What type of mission are you giving me now Archangel Michael? You initiated me for eighteen daily months, preparing me to detox him and bring him back to life in a healthy body. Nourishing him and giving him supplements, organic food, and clean water and now he is back into these psychotropic drugs? and seven different ones.

It makes no sense. Allison seems also to have been attacked again and is sick. Allison is my agent and once the cabal found out that she was working for me she fell into a mysterious 2-month coma. She was doing much better, but all communication stopped six days ago.

Three days later I received "New opportunities are on the way or that this is the start of a new beginning." A Spanish researcher found a way to remove magnetic graphene from the body after a COVID-JAB. He successfully tested an inexpensive way to remove magnetic graphene nano-particles from the human body after they were injected via COVID-19 vaccination.

Using Glutathione (1 capsule in the morning) or N-Acetylcysteine, zinc, Vit. D3, Quercetin 5mg, Astaxanthin, milk thistle (radioactive protection), and melatonin at night for 2 weeks.

CHAPTER 14
The Implementation of Transhumanism

I was so exhausted that the minute I closed my eyes, I fell into a deep sleep, and I began to receive some information. It was coming from a deep and warm male voice before then it was shown to me in a movie on a huge screen.

"We are living inside a highly advanced computer simulation where people remember details of various names and quotes that differ from the current reality. Some time ago negative forces arrived on Earth."

That is where the visions began to appear.

"They used advanced mind control techniques to take over the planet's inhabitants and seized control of the Earth's resources. The negative forces and currently trying to take over the entire galaxy. These dark and evil creatures can also disguise themselves as humans and it makes it very difficult, they hide in plain sight.

That is how human beings became hackable animals with the push toward transhumanism and the technology that is required to make humans controllable. With the monitoring of the bodies and thoughts potentially transmitted into a vast database from where the information could eventually be integrated with

AI. It is through nanotechnology like microscopic machines within the bodies that the implantation of transhumanism can be accomplished. These microscopic machines can transmit radio signals and alter human DNA. And the agenda of these evil creatures is to reduce the size of the population for more control and have surveillance of other megacities. Everything is good enough for them to reduce the population, by infertility, and chemical castration to stop human reproduction. Getting many human beings to think that there is an overpopulation.

But there is good news. The Earth will be restored and healed, there will be no more darkness. The Earth will ascend to a higher frequency where evil creatures cannot access and live. The Earth will be a Galactic Federation Planet again. The Planet was once part of that group but became disconnected.

A Hundred million years ago the Galactic Federation was founded for an essential reason, to assist planet Earth in its transition out of deep space and back into the Galactic Federation status. And that will also help the expansion of human consciousness, and it will help us to understand the truth about how special the planet is.

The people on Earth will choose to ascend with the ascension process from the third to a much higher frequency of the fifth dimension and will do so along with the planet.

Ascension means that humanity will no longer be living in denial and will begin to live as one in harmony with each other and the natural world. As more souls wake up, they will start embracing their Divinity by looking inward for guidance and stop relying on outer authorities or the media.

Earth will transform into a lush paradise of abundant lifeforms, clean air, and sparkling water. The Erath inhabitants will have to rise above the lower vibrational frequencies of fear and judgment and live in peace, harmony, and light in their hearts. This high frequency will affect humans physically and spiritually as they transform from a more carbon-based physical structure to a crystalline-based one. All these things are predicted to occur, and all that is part of a divine plan!

As full members now of the Galactic Federation planet, every soul on Earth will have access to technology that makes life more enjoyable and easier. Anti-gravity devices, cold fusion energy devices, and advanced teleportation systems."

Wow! And this was it for that day.

CHAPTER 15

The Symbol will be their downfall

Two months later my Friend named Fannie introduced me to a Hollywood whistleblower. She looked at me for a while straight in the eyes before she finally spoke and said:

"I need you to spread this information. The Symbolism of Snow-White Death. The Cabal has to let you be aware of their action, and their agenda before it happens.

So, they used Hollywood with the Snow-White movies. The seven dwarfs were cabal satellites that were replaced with star links.

The Cabal has been taken down and replaced. I know that you can't talk about it, you will not be

heard but write about it." Symbols carry different meanings. Some Pentacles are related to the devil.

The symbolism of the feminine pentacle is correct, but the symbolism of the pentacle has been distorted over the millennia.

And that was confirmed by the Galactic through a message they sent me:

The present time is crucial in human history. The dark forces' reign is coming to an end. They've used up all their might and control over you. they have exhausted their power, and they can no longer harm Earth. They are clinging to their power. This is the time to break free of the chains of darkness.

Life is a journey; it is a series of problems. The real problem is not the problem itself but our attitude towards it. Bless it and observe the change.

Here is a Suggested Practice

"I thank Thee, Father God, for …… may it/they …… be Blessed and welcome Thy peace."

CHAPTER 16
The Last Communication with Allison

It was on Friday, December 16, late in the morning that I received a text from my agent Allison. This was the last time I received anything from her.

"Good morning, VIE! Thank you for continuously sending me healing energies. I sincerely apologize, my body was consumed by darkness again and I was unconscious for days.

I am currently still unable to move freely but I will send you all the audio and review your email as soon as I can do so.

Please contact me and pray for complete healing. I do not want to be eaten raw from inside by the dark side. I am afraid, VIE.

Please contact me by email as my phone is acting up. Reptilians are weakening my spirit and body. I am really frightened that I won't make it. I will be sending all the files to Crown later today. I will keep you posted." -Allison

Then silence.

On Sunday, March 5, at lunchtime EST, I received an e-mail from her sister that time, saying:

"Hello Ms. VIE,

I hope all is well with you and your family. This is the sister of Allison. I just recently got access to all her online accounts and work email.

I am deeply saddened to inform you that my beloved sister did not make it. She passed away and joined our creator earlier in the morning on Friday, March 3, after battling her "illnesses" for months. After being in a coma for months, she had a cerebral Hemorrhage this morning which she, unfortunately, did not survive.

She was always talking about you. She kept telling us that your work deserves to be shared as it helped her feel good.

She left a note letting you know that she will be watching your presentation and success from above. She mentioned a name for you to contact to continue what she left behind. I would like to thank you for healing my sister even for a short period. She's lucky to have worked with someone like you. Please continue to help and heal a lot of sick people. Veronica Medard"

That is when I remembered clearly a few years ago these AI insects that were crawling in my brain and my body until my spiritual family took care of them. I had so many, and it could only be cleaned three to five per week. It took one year to clean it all. It has to be encapsulated one by one. It would have broken my body and would not have been able to survive it. It was too poisonous. That was what Allison was referring to in her last text on December 16, she sent me. That's what killed her when she had the cerebral Hemorrhage. The Reptilians killed her.

And I would like to add in remembrance and gratitude for Allison's work and courage. She dared to do her mission work till the end. She never backs up in the face of dark energies. She was an angel on earth and had the time to leave a note so that I could continue my work and mission for the planet.

Please readers get out of your comfort zone and do your mission, or you will end up the same way.

Whistleblowers, the courageous people, are killed one by one, in the same way, to help human beings to survive and go to the golden age. They are killed in different, and various ways. A missing millionaire was found dead and chopped up in a suitcase. And there are many others killed brutally. Some lately are pushed out the windows from the fifth floor or attacked during their sleep unable to defend themselves as they are not ready or by lack of knowledge. Christians are killed for their faith in Jesus. And so much more is going on while you choose to ignore it and call the awakened and helpers "completists or conspirators" Did you know that your rice contains arsenic? And snake venom in vaccines and your foods, there are six thousand patents suppressed technologies. The news is fake, the war is real.

Time to wake up! Do not stay trapped in the matrix, or you will be accountable for not doing your job. For not having taken part in the battle. Stop being sheep.

CHAPTER 17

A Thought Thrown At VIE; CHADD Gets Some Help.

This occurred when I was browsing a big market full of exotic and natural products when a woman approached me. She was tall. Slim with green eyes dark hair and a nice suntan completion. In a very weird island accent, she told me her name was Kalani, and in a nearly inaudible voice said, "I was waiting for you" She looked like coming from another time, or another world if you prefer. I was wondering if she was real or if I was having a vision. But Kalani continued.

"Each step on a journey is different; chaos is a temporary phase between one natural state of harmony and its transformation into a higher form

Today, we are in a storm before the calm. Chaos is a temporary phase between one natural state of harmony and its transformation into a higher form. The transition phase between the two states becomes very rough until the higher form is reached

Humanity must awaken now. With the holographic movie projection world people are trapped in the matrix, and many people are dying

As you know CHADD decided to come to this world and take the pain of others. But he never thought it would be so ugly, and it would turn out to this extent to his body. His body has been much more damaged than you think. He is being sent help for the regeneration of his body and what is necessary to fight disease, because he has more work to do

And you VIE, you have today wounds behind your ear and in three places in your back of the time when you were stabbed to death once. It's psychic scars coming back. You see it is another thing that no one knows. One of the designs put in the COVID is to connect with the souls' past. This Covid-19 is linked to the past. When you died you were stabbed in the back and under your ears

Then later you had stomach problems. Invisible dark forces attacked you. A thought ball was thrown at you. They have put a harsh intent in a circle and thrown it infecting your solar plexus and your knees. They do not want you to succeed and be rewarded for your work. They try to weaken and discomfort your body. They forced open the sphincter valve in your body that does not close, and the valve let's all get back up in the throat".

The Message was given and Kalani disappeared. The Dark forces understood that our trials and tribulations were ending and that they had to leave Earth. They knew they were losing control and did not want to go but had to. So, they created chaos, hurt, pain, and many other bad things before being forced to leave. Like the change in human DNA. They try hard to stop humanity from taking their Light body.

CHAPTER 18
CHADD Psychiatric GemsCamp, the Stone Center Evaluation Event

Finally, the time had arrived. Well! I thought. After 17 years of battle, the forced ingestion of drug prescriptions ended. Unfortunately, this will only be for a short period.

I shook my head. I took a deep breath and tried to calm down. Is it just a dream, I said. I awoke and looked around. I stared a moment longer to finally sit on the bed.

That is when communication between us started my day. And a vision appeared. I could not keep my eyes off the scene. CHADD was seated next to the surrogate hybrid Katherine in a doctor's office and in front of Dr. Jazlin Estampery. The exact same one that without seeing CHADD prescribed him many times dangerous drugs like Zanex with terrible side effects. And made him grind his teeth. The same drugs that killed one of Betsy's patients.

I gaze up, two monks are here staring below in my direction. It's an inevitable prophecy said one of the monks. When health is subverted into just one more commercial cycle of worsening food, new diseases, and more drugs, Armageddon is the result. Psychiatric patients are treated as human guinea pigs:

When CHADD tells his story, it sounds more like a conspiracy than his tragic past. But many of the details are laid out in thick files of docs. They gave him all the drugs they could available. The idea of mind control, the theory that breaking a person down will make them do something against their will, has been constantly revisited by the government during other periods of fear and uncertainty when the military and medicine collide. But that day he decided to end it. He knew the psychiatric doctor Jazlin was not expecting it.

Dr. Jazlin Estampery: See the pattern CHADD? I never gave much thought to what it would be like. She paused for a moment. It is important to understand how it works.

She was trying to get its trust but did not expect what was coming. CHADD stared at Dr. Estampery for a moment before saying: I am here to tell you that I will not take any more of your drugs. I refuse and will not continue to let my body be poisoned.

Dr. Estamper: But I have never seen anything like this before. Well! In that case, I have to send you seventy-two hours for evaluation.

CHADD had a smile and replied: I repeat I will not ingest any of your drugs. I am a doctor. I am the Doctor of Sound.

But Dr. Estamper ignored him, she glanced around in a moment of reflection, then decided to baker act him.

That happened on Friday, March 17 in the afternoon. The Police came, put CHADD in one of their cars, and drove him to the Stone Center Psychiatric Hospital. At dinner time, he had his first meal with his menu. On the very top of the menu was the list of all foods he was allergic to red dye 40, shellfish, iodine. And the very first meal contained the three of them.

During the night CHADD awakens not feeling well at all. Scratching and bleeding. The second day CHADD awakened his eyes and his tongue swelling. He asked the nurses for help, but they ignored him. At dinner time they gave him again some red dye 40 for his food. At that time the hospital nurses gave him an anti-inflammatory pill. But just before bed gave him a red pill with red dye 40 in it that he refused, and they switched it for a white pill. On the third day, CHADD was given lunch with some shellfish he was allergic to. His face got swollen and his eyes were so swollen he had to put compress after compress.

It came Monday morning and I began to be very worried. I did not hear from him, and it was unusual.

My phone rang and it was him. How come you are able to call me from your phone I said. Well! He said laughing, they have tried to kill me since Friday. All weekend, Saturday, and Sunday I kept saying the name of my attorney again, and again, telling out loud attempting murder. This will cost a lot. All of a sudden this morning I was called to the front of the reception desk, and I was told that I was released.

A nurse guided me out and put me in an Uber car. She gave me a sandwich with peanut butter and jelly which contains red dye 40. She pushed me inside the car and sent me home. I was asked to never come back, and I was released without any prescription drugs.

On Friday Afternoon I came to Dr. Jazlin Estamp's office with the surrogate driving my car equipped with push-pull hands-control. I had to take a course and pass a test to be able to drive it.

As I was baker acted and was brought to the Gem Center psychiatric hospital in a police car, the surrogate had to go back home. Alone. She did not leave the car parked and called for transportation. No, but she drove my car without insurance or a license to drive it, and she is diabetic. She can't see well or ear well anymore with her sickness. Getting out of the Uber vehicle I found my car parked with many scratches on the outside of the driver's door, but luckily for Katherine, she wasn't arrested and did not get into an accident.

One week later, Karma or the law of the universe, the following consequences of an act caught Katherine. She woke up with Covid and lost four teeth.

But archons never learn their lessons I thought. She tried again to have CHADD into drugs. Ten days passed and I found a text on my phone: "Mrs. Katherine you will have to reschedule the appointment you made for CHADD. Dr. Estampery is out of office."

But like I said the drug's prescription stopped but not for long and she reappeared after Katherine told me in an arrogant tone of voice "he wanted his freedom? see what happens now."

CHAPTER 19
When Problems Indicate A New Vibration
is Coming

The Archangels are knocking on my door today and they're bringing me an important message.

"Problems always indicate a turn of the wave and of a new vibration that pertains to your destiny. What happened to CHADD is one example of it.

Unfortunately, Katherine and her son Paul, the hybrids, refuse to turn to the light. They work, worship, and serve the devil.

First let me tell you that: Our Body Appears to be Separated, but actually, is an Extensions of the Cosmos. Growing up you were told to discriminate. to see the differences between you and others. You are taught to label people, superior or inferior, friends or opponents and you are also taught to label yourself. It creates duality and millions are killed in the name of religion, caste, nation, color, and gender.

The truth is that everything is one in union with the Cosmos. The Divine is within you and not far from you. The Divine and the individual are one and not two separate things. This is why you must refrain from harming others.

Non-violence is not just a method of achieving political and economic objectives, it is a way of life.

The contrary of violence is love, sympathy, and service coupled with sacrifice and suffering to bring about a change for good in the opponent. It holds that evil can be conquered by love, and darkness can be dissipated by light. It is like there is nothing wrong with children having ADD. They do not need or deserve to be put on "medications"

I was guided through a glowing tunnel into the brilliant white Light on the other side of the tunnel. And I saw the biggest fear of the World Economic Forum is that you will make your decision, and you will not follow their orders. They want to destroy what cannot be controlled. So, they are talking about a series of injections. that is the absolute key because without it they can't control your life. They cannot mandate that you do something without it.

CHAPTER 20

Seven Days at Point Rocks Hospital Naked

CHADD and I were having lunch when he decided to share with me and said "Katherine, her son Paul, and his son Alexander Hybrids refuse to turn to the light. They are seen as three circles, one next to the other.

They work and worship the devil, and by the law of karma, they will have to leave the consequences of it." Proverb 6:2 teaches that you are trapped by the words of your mouth.

"They reported twisted news to control, separate, and divide to control us, VIE. One week later Katherine had failed her kidneys. Already two weeks earlier she lost four teeth due to the same attitude. But now being weaker and weaker she involved Paul."

CHADD was brought by the police for seven days at the Point of Rocks Hospital naked and transferred stripped of his clothes, prescription glasses, and his pinky gold ring to a reevaluation center for 3 more days an hour from his home.

CHADD invited a man he just met, who pretended to have no place to live. He invited the man to sleep in the coach. Upon the man entering the house Paul reached for his gun and pointed it at the man's temple saying, You get out of my house right now or I blow your fucking mind, and CHADD was thrown in the street with him. What CHADD did not know was that the man was an instrument of evil forces to get him in trouble. For a while, these evil forces were sending CHADD some paid people trying to get him into problems.

So, after being kicked out they went out for dinner. They went to a restaurant that pretended to know the new man and invited them to it for free. But after the meal, the owner of the restaurant presented them with a bill. They could not pay, and CHADD was issued a restrictive order and a date to go to court, but he never was served the legal paper. They both hung around all night and in the morning the police came and arrested the man. CHADD was left alone in the street in his wheelchair, with no money for twenty more hours until the police came and transported him to a Ceremonial hospital for seven days where he was stripped of all his clothes, belongings, and even his Cartier prescription glasses, then driven to Point Rocks Hospital. After CHADD called home to ask Katherine to bring him some clothes, not only did he never receive any cloth, but the nurse told him confidentially that Katherine bypassed the Hospital Doctor in charge and called saying that he needed a psychotropic drug injection of Aldol. She pretended to have the power of attorney from a judge, but no one ever saw this power of attorney. That she denied having afterward. But CHADD received the injection and against his will of course. Imagine! Aldol is a kind of crack cocaine.

CHADD was finally driven back home. Katherine made clear that he had an appointment three days later with Jazlin Estamper for a prescription and he would have to obey her and take it or he would be thrown again in the street. Then Katherine called Paul and asked him to contact my family to make sure that there would not be any more communication between them, or he would take care of it

Wow! Controlling by fear. Paul reported some fake twisted information and lies, and I became controlled by my family controlled my fears. I was told that I would be left in the street if I ever would communicate again with CHADD.

A few months earlier my spiritual family told me that two of CHADD's family were gone and three more would be removed. Katherine, Paul, and his son. All Hybrids and dark energies.

Here we are the time is approaching. Tiktok! Tiktok! But Paul went even further in his control. Knowing that CHADD is in a wheelchair and to get out of the house he has to close the first door to open the second and get to the ramp he installed a timing device of five seconds. Which is leaving CHADD trapped in the house.

Two weeks later, as if it was not enough, Katherine who gets sicker and sicker each passing day, forced CHADD to ingest psychotropic drugs but gave him to swallow an overdose of these pills. It was Monday morning around eleven when my phone rang. I did not recognize the phone number but saw the same area as CHADD's. I picked it up ready to hear who it was. And it was Him. Still very cautious knowing how vicious these hybrids are when I heard his voice I rapidly said, I could not talk and just before I hung up the phone, I heard I was at the hospital. I immediately called back the number and that is what I heard.

"I was released when I heard he was going to be ok without permanent damage." That is where I finally received the answer to my longtime wondering How come Katherine has authority over Banker Managers, Social Security Department, Doctors in Hospitals, and Judges in Court? This Hybrid woman sold CHADD to the state in exchange for immunity.

WOW! So, Katherine has immunity, Paul has a link with the corrupt people he worked with in the State, and Alex the maffoso. Tiktok! Tiktok! Time is Ticking.

CHAPTER 21

Reunion with Eleana

That long-time friend, after years without communication, suddenly reappeared in my life. She was sent to help the God Duo.

It was on a Friday at about lunchtime. The phone rang and I heard "I am here at the airport. I will stay in your state for a few days. I would like to see you".

Eleana? Is it you I said he took me by surprise. I began to remember the beautiful eyes she had and how she was always a joy for her friend to be around.

Great! I said, "Where are you staying? She replied, in a hotel not too far from you. Then I asked her how she was going to get to her hotel. Have you some kind of transportation, asked. I did not know if someone was waiting for her, and she said "Well, I guess the hotel can pick me up, they must have a transformation" Wait for me Eleana, I said, I am coming to pick you up."

I was worried wondering if I would recognize her. It has been so long since we saw each other. I arrived at the airport and parked just in front of a woman with an adorable little service dog in her arms and four enormous suitcases plus many small bags.

I stood there staring at the woman until Eleana broke the staring silence and said "So, you are not going to give me a hug?" At that same time, a man in his thirties grabbed one of the luggage and began to load it into my car. Luckily I was driving a 4WD Atlas.

That is where my navigation system decided to drive all around town to reach her hotel instead of taking the highway. But we finally arrived, and she insisted on taking a quick shower before we could go and have dinner together,

The A/C was not functioning correctly and what I thought would be a quick shower turned out to be ninety minutes and me waiting in my car outside. We finally headed towards a restaurant and did not see the time passing by, I still had to drive back to my house and went to bed at one in the morning. But this was the beginning of a reunion for our missions.

Eleana, I was convinced that she was sent to help the God Duo. And I was right when I finally heard the name of the real Judge of Justice. The one that rules by the Laws of the Constitution. Then I heard CHADD telling me that she had been sent to us purposely.

CHAPTER 22

You are the Light That Refused To Surrender

I had a very intense day at the convention center. I feel a little bit dizzy. I saw and spoke to so many people. Here I am now finally in my hotel room. I lay down and fall asleep for a short time, then I wake up. But I am so tired I fall asleep again, over and over. I do not want to miss any information I am receiving.

The reality in which we live is so different from what most people think of it. They hang on the past references. But the world is changing. People think and talk about "Completism" or science fiction when it is not. The awakening may be hard for them.

We live in a world of AI, and disinformation. Yes, fish fall from the sky, Spirit slips out of the body to commit murder.

Well knowns supercenters, and one-stop grocery stores in multiple cities across the US are being used as Camps, and Global warming is a scam. I glanced at the clock. and it says "History is happening. Don't waste any more time, the truth is coming. She thinks that you are kidding right?"

In the middle of a long deep dream, I try to breathe slowly, and the scene continues. Inevitably karma is coming. How dare they think of separating the God Duo!

CHADD whispers in my ear: God will recall her soon. She went too far. She refused to go to the light. I told you many times VIE; I will be free when she passes away. But the time she went too far. She and Paul and his son hate you.

Suddenly I began to feel the warmth and peacefulness. I took a breath with my eyes closed and perceived an unusual, sweet fragrance like a bouquet of fresh-cut flowers. I opened my eyes and looked but there were no flowers close by. I understood I was receiving a message, and I thought something was happening.

Indeed. The surrogate was sick and felt the need to have her corrupted son Paul, also an archon to take over. She managed to report in her own words, and she interpreted what she listened to. What could she have heard from CHADD's phone call with VIE? As she only heard part of the phone calls, she decided to tell her own story from it. Telling Paul that I was going to run away with CHADD to Arizona. This was their biggest fear. They will not be able then to control him anymore, get his Government check, and baker act him to keep him on psychotropic drugs. They would lose authority.

Katherine decided to make also an appointment with Jazlin Estamp, but she got so sick that she had to cancel the appointment. But it did not last, Heals! Paul installed cameras in every room of the house. There is no privacy at all, not even in the bathrooms. But it did not last a terrible storm destroyed the entire system.

We have been, CHADD and I, stolen from so many years of our lives to help you. And we love you and we bless you. May you awaken quickly and make it to the Fifth.

CHAPTER 23

GOD Answer

As soon as I woke up and walked down the hall I entered a vortex and traveled to another place. A place from where I see we are being challenged by world events. Whether we like it or not, life today is different in ways we never expected, we are challenged to grow and to love.

The pineal gland is a spiritual organ destined to be a connecting link between the human and the divine and its function has been kept hidden and for most calcified by all the toxicities.

It looks like the golden age will come when the sun, moon, and Jupiter all meet in the same quadrant as the Tisha constellation, which is part of Cancer.

CHADD is VIE tainted angel and hero. He went through so much for you. He was many times poisoned and beaten, they did some unnecessary surgeries while he was in a coma after an overdose of psychotropic drugs he was forced to ingest for forty-four years, left in a wheelchair handicapped. They destroyed his image, made a fool of him, deprived him of identity and freedom, used him as a guinea pig, was never retributed and so much more. He had no one that cared enough to help him. Not the family, of course, they sold him at the age of six to the state, not the neighbors cared, and neither the Pastor he considered a "friend" was..

VIE decided to ask for help directly from the father. With Paul monitoring CHADD's phone and looking at the cameras to make sure CHADD and VIE would not communicate this was beginning to be too much.

And this Sunday morning this is what the Father guided me to read in the Bible. Look at what it says:

Isaiah 59:15-16

15- "Truth is nowhere to be found, and whoever shuns evil becomes a prey. The LORD looked and was displeased that there was no justice".

16- "He saw that there was no one, he was appalled that there was no one to intervene; so, his own arm achieved salvation for him, and his own righteousness sustained him".

Truth is nowhere to be found, and whoever shuns evil becomes prey. The LORD looked and was displeased that there was no justice.
He saw that there was no one; he was appalled that there was no one to intervene; so, his own arm achieved salvation for him, and his own righteousness sustained him.

CHAPTER 24

Emma and the Emissary

On a Monday afternoon, a couple were sent to meet me. One young girl, Emma, and the second Mark the messenger. I entered the Library and looked around the different shelves of books. I was reading the different books' titles and writers' names when a young woman asked me if I also was one. One what, did I reply? A fairy, she said.

And we began to talk for about thirty minutes until she received a phone call and left me saying it was nice talking to you my friend just arrived I have to go. And she left. I grabbed a few books and walked towards a table in the cafe.

Looking around for a quiet table, I found out that the only table left in a corner was next to the Fairy woman. She immediately introduced me to the man with blue eyes, that called himself an Emissary.

The Emissary man grabbed a chair and came to sit at my round table. He started the conversation by telling me that he was struck out by the lightning and had received some gifts and visions. He also explained that he was a devoted Catholic and was a Jesus follower. Said that he was sent to visit hell as a witness to be able to tell people that Hell exists and described what he saw. But I did not stay as you can tell, he said.

He saw some strange creatures, and some of these still lived underground. He saw some dragons with twelve heads and a friend had recently passed away. He described the pit of hell as a big whole with no end. Like an infinite funnel.

Emma the fairy and her friend Emissionary did not have a car, so I asked Emisionary if he lived far. He replied a little embarrassed with a vague gesture that his father dropped him here, but he was guided to come to this library because he needed to meet me.

While this conversation was taking place Emma was trying to resolve her problem on the phone with her bank.

She made a deposit in cash a few days earlier, but the ATM refused to give her cash, and the cashier was not able to give her some cash giving her. As an excuse for her protection, and to come back in thirty days then the funds would be accessible.

I offered to give her a drive to a branch, and she gladly accepted. When she came out of the bank I saw by the expression on her face that something happened. Emma the fairy woman with purple hair got back in the car, looked at me, and asked me "Are the bank employees robots now, because they act like it?"

Then I received the vision.

"Be prepared for the ultimate shockwave.

We are now witnesses to an epic battle an unprecedented series of events, masterfully orchestrated according to the Laws of War. The banking system is changing for the better, and the people's Freedom, but the bankers of the old banking system are resisting the change, and they are withholding their clients' money.

US incorporations have been dissolved due to the demise of their fiat Federal Reserve US Dollar and a global Financial Collapse that was now in the works. A global Currency Reset based on gold asset-based currencies of 209 nations is soon to be complete. There would be a restoration of the US government to the New Republic based on the fundamentals of the original Constitution. For now, 27 States have agreed to join the New Republic which was said to be based in Texas. Hawaii should revert to its original status as a sovereign nation. Canada, Mexico, Australia, and New Zealand have asked to Join.

Am I given a hint about the changeover to the New US Republic thanks to Alisa?
Emma came back to say thanks, bye, nice meeting you. I saw her crossing the road and
she disappeared.

CHAPTER 25
The Feminine Principle Wisdom and The Invisible Infinite Light

Mia, a good friend of mine that I met while traveling in Singapore decided to quit her job to travel the world.

She was on a quest for a new sense of personal destiny and purpose. She was raised Roman Catholic and did not know what to think anymore. She needed to understand.

She went to France to Sainte Mary de la Mer. That was what she felt she had to go to first.

Before the visitation to France, she could not have accepted the gift she was going to receive.

Mia entered the Monastery and was led to a very large room with high ceilings and into a smaller room on the other side, in which six monks were praying.

She found out that Mary Magdalene is the one who unites the opposite without obliterating. Mary Magdalene holds the worlds together and is often represented by holding a jar of balm for healing as well as anointing the dead.

She discovered that the Catholic Church should not be called Roman but Gallican Catholic Church, and the Gallican Catholic and Apostolic Churches were completely different from the Roman Catholics. They never impose, or judge. They do not excommunicate.

They teach the word of God and guide people to Him, to the best of their knowledge.

She says that she learned that Sophia is the feminine Principle of wisdom. The Holy Spirit. One is the invisible infinite Light the self-awareness, Trinity. And the Son is Christ the anointed.

Holy Spirit, Sophia is the feminine counterpart of Christ. Both Archetypes are unified in a Sacred Marriage within the Trinity.

Walking around the monastery wanting to learn as much as she could, she discovered a post on the power of love and about who Mary Magdalene is.

The power of love. Love is the highest vibration in the universe, and it can heal all wounds and transcend all limitations. By cultivating love and compassion, humans can evolve to higher levels of consciousness and connect with the universal consciousness.

Mary Magdalene is the Holy Grail. She is the Mother of the Royal bloodline of Jesus Christ. Mary Magdalene was the womb that carried the Royal lineage.

Mary Magdalene is the one who unites the opposite with not obligatory either.

Then Mia said, "Suddenly as I traveled to another world, I felt a range of sensations. I became light-headed and was projected off the Earth plane. A sense of rapture coursed through me. I realized I was being anointed by Mary Magdalene. My quest was over. I had to carry the message.

It may look a little bit complicated, but this is what I found out after being anointed The Anunnaki, which are the Cabal, the controllers, and the actual Government came to Earth seeking gold to repair their ozone layer. The Anunnaki's reliance on technology and their current wars caused them to lose touch with cosmic consciousness.

The High-Frequency Active Aurora Research in Alaska made us aware of the potential for affecting the climate in many ways. This has been entrusted to the Anunnaki in charge of the weather. Secret military science and technology, through various means, can raise the temperature or trigger bursts, lightning and storms to break out clouds.

Thus, the atmosphere and climate, the land, and the sea were all monitored to create a terrible drought that was to decimate or destroy mankind.

The Anunnaki came to Earth from Niburu seeking gold to repair their ozone layer. The Anunnaki reliance on technology and their recurrent wars caused them to lose touch with cosmic consciousness."

MIA came back home, and she is now carrying the message to as many people and in as many ways as she can, and more specifically to the "Roman" Catholics who like her try to make some sense to be able to continue to worship and follow the Father.

CHAPTER 26

Could the Brain-Machine be the Mark of the Beast?

I am feeling so good this early summer morning.

It is so beautiful. I am feeling so much love. My left ear is rigging. It is communication with the source giving me healing instructions.

The Bible in Revelation 13:16-18 says 16 Also it causes all, both small and great, both rich and poor, both free and slave, to be marked on the right hand or the forehead, 17 so that no one can buy or sell unless he has the mark, that is, the name of the beast or the number of its name. 18 This calls for wisdom: let him who has understanding reckon the number of the beast, for it is a human number, its number is six hundred and sixty-six.

Receiving a mark on the right hand, or the forehead. Hum! Does it look like brain-phone implants imposed by the Cabals to take over our brain, and control us?

And if we look again at 1 Corinthians 3:16-17 it says:

"Do you not know that you are the temple of God and that the spirit of God dwells in you? If anyone defiles the temple of God, God will destroy him. For the temple of God is Holy which you are."

Many people often find themselves caught up in their daily routine on autopilot without taking the time to reflect on their lives and the world around them.

Without any real sense of purpose or direction. But by cultivating awareness and embracing the present moment, they can tap into the container of wisdom and insight and lead toward enlightenment.

The quest for enlightenment, and awareness, is the key to unlocking the door. Awareness allows you to see beyond the physical realm and into the deeper, spiritual dimension of existence. It is the doorway to transformation, the path to enlightenment, and the key to unlocking the secrets of the universe.

Remember that the awakening process is a natural part of humanity's evolution. You are contributing to the creation and the evolution of each of the collective conscious.

The internet was designed for the US Department to communicate after a nuclear war. After inserting a smartphone inside your brain, your brain will work like a computer. You will enter an alternative reality. Your real world and the virtual world will feel the same.

You will search and click just by thinking. You will see the screen even though it is not there. You will drop-down menus, listen to music, look at movies, and make purchases. Brain phones, the mark of the beast, will ruin personalities, communities, and our bodies.

What you must remember is that governments and corporations exist to take advantage of you and control you. Your thoughts will easily be transmitted and stored. Once the brain machine is inserted and up and running, This network will be controlled by one powerful entity. To transform this world into hell. AI is designed to enter and destroy our world.

The fifth Dimension is a state of consciousness that has been locked away in the human mind for thousands of years.

CHAPTER 27

The Backdrop People

A woman dressed in a long robe and with angel wings appeared, came towards me, and said:

"VIE many people are stopping the light. You must increase yours. Certain groups try to stop your light from doing what you are here to do. People on Earth are against each other and changes cannot be made."

I see myself now behind a desk, I wave my hand and a holographic symbol comes up floating, in front of me and on top of the desk. I stretch my hand and put it over it, and it makes an interesting tone. I move around different symbols suspended above it. The feminine angel laughed at my face and said, "The purpose of it is to travel to another place. It takes off, out of the room and I am following it. It has become light, and I am creating. I am excited as I am learning to create.

Backdrops of people are holographic images. They look solid but they are not. The attention of people makes them real. But if you talk to these people you would not tell the difference. Backdrop people are not alive, but the amount of people given to them at some point gives them the chance to be real. Backdrops are holographic people. They are just images that get activated by the attention given to them by others.

Otherwise, they are only motion picture images. They do not have a soul and are without higher-self. If you interact with one, even if you touched one, you would not know the difference, and you are surrounded by many."

CHAPTER 28
You Are the Architect of Your Reality

I am dreaming again. It seems to be rushing water ahead. The sun is shining brightly, and I am lying there on the grass. There are wonderful flowers of radiant colors and glorious music. I can see in my mind's eye a group of people sitting around a room. They are anxious to participate and hear about the subject.

There is a rainbow to remind us of the color of energy and creation. it's just a reminder, there is way more than we can see with just the naked eye. The color of creation is all of various colors, that are beyond the visualization of human beings. This is a reminder of home and of the loving energy and that there was a time when this energy wrapped around us in another realm. We are reminded there is more to the spectrum of color than we see with the naked eye. That we are all connected. We are all one and multidimensional spiritual beings having first an experience.

I see coming to me through the flowers a beautiful woman with dark long hair, and brown eyes, she is wearing a long gown and looks radiant and beautiful. I believe I communicate with my higher self. Am I? She is talking to me.

"I have contacted you because you are going to talk to them and let this group of people hear what they came to hear. They are here to understand that they are the architect of their reality and must awaken to their true nature. They are powerful Creators and do not know it."

Then, I entered telepathic communication with CHADD. After a short introduction of myself to the group I began to give the lecture they came to hear.

"You have chosen to incarnate on this beautiful planet Terra Christa to be part of a grand tapestry of creation and each one of you is a high-energy being. You are an emissary of light with the ability from the quantum level to the dream level. You are a sparks creator in your own right bringing forth the imagination of all that is and all can be at times it can seem challenging.

At this very moment in history is ripe with potential and purpose, it is through your deliberate choices and conscious actions that you can transform the world around you.

Feel the resonance of the collection consciousness pulsating with dreams desires and intentions of every living being. You are an integral part of this cosmic symphony.

A vital thread is interwoven, with the fabric of existence from the quantum level where particles dance in perfect harmony to the dream level where possibilities unfurl. You have the power to mold reality. Your thoughts intentions and actions are energetic seeds ready to blossom into the most beautiful creations. Embrace the truth you are. The weavers of destiny. The masters of creation. Embrace the calling of your soul, for it knows the path that led to joy, abundance, and fulfillment.

In this journey of self-discovery and co-creation, perceived limitations are mere illusions designed to test you. Every challenge you encounter is an opportunity for growth and an invitation to step into your true power. Trust in the resilience of your spirit for you are capable of miracles far beyond measure. Embrace the beauty of diversity. Extend your love, kindness, and compassion to all beings you encounter in your journey for they also are Divine Expression of consciousness. Let your intentions be aligned with harmony and let your actions be guided by wisdom. Embrace the Cosmic dance of creation and watch in awe as the world transforms."

CHAPTER 29
Shape-Shifters, Spirit that Possesses Others, and Visualizations for Protection

I met several shapeshifters. One day I was at the bank next to a man in his forties. The man was in front of a very beautiful and attractive young cashier. It was when I saw the man's face shape-shifting and changing into a monster.

The second time took me also by surprise. I was at the walking center for a CHADD that had food poisoning. I Knew for a few years this Indian woman and had no idea. Many people from the neighborhood knew her for her service. Looking at CHADD she suddenly shaped-shifter into a demonic person while saying you look too white for me. I cannot do anything for you.

I heard of incidents lately that create fear for the public. The reptilians are not even trying to hide anymore. They know they have lost the battle. They have raped young girls and children, sodomized young boys, controlled humanity for thousands of years, killed, tortured made adrenochrome from alive children from their blood, they have eaten human flesh, and it is time it comes to an end.

Some entities have simply not evolved, and they are entities that can be considered demonic and possess others. Possession is an elemental overtaking. They are elemental on Earth Spirit. They are fed upon emotions of hate and lust.

When someone is possessed it is a warped spirit on a level of demons. They are lower than human souls and they have been warped through touch or contact by certain entities, or by people so that they can bend and evil. Those possessions are caused by someone who usually has disorganized energy.

The reason they enter this body is that it has been seriously imbalanced. Many actual cases are people on psychotropic drugs, they become a magnet to them. They do not have their act and violence ensues. The violent actions are the result. Drugs are demons and give a false feeling, causing major addiction to the DNA that is compromised, making you spiritually vulnerable at this point.

White light is very effective in exorcising, and it is effective for protection when dealing with people whose auras seem to conflict with yours.

If a person is aware of being overtaken, all that must say is "I command you to leave in the name of Jesus" The person has to obey this name, she has no other choice but to leave.

Here is a very effective visualization for protection given to me for you to practice: See yourself enveloped in a pyramid of brilliant white Light energy surrounding and surrounding the building you are in, or whatever you feel will work for you. "I Ask that all discreative energies within the transformed and aligned into the creative of the Universe" and "I ask that the discreative energy which causes the manifestation of illness, be burned to the white Light, and aligned and turned Back to the Universe in a creative manner." Anyone can create a pyramid of white Light and surround themselves with it.

Energy can't be destroyed, but it can be converted from negative to positive. Any discreative energies that come near the pyramid will be returned to be transformed into constructive ones and recycled.

CHAPTER 30

KARMA is a Cycle You Have Generated

I am asleep. At first, I was not aware of having a body but seemed to be floating. Then I find myself in a room with beings of light. They are greeting me. They are just magnificent beings of light. They are not judgemental; they just guide and suggest. They say: "Life should be walked in Light and kindness. Let the healing begin"

"People do not understand. They are the Light and they refused to surrender. But one cannot go to the new Earth until it has finished paying Karma. They can't move on until you repay it. They have to let it go.

This is probably the cause of illness and of all their problems holding onto all the baggage and all that they carry with them. If they have been mistreated when they were young or have been beaten by their husband it does not matter. One must let it go.

You have to forgive; You have to release. This is it or you will not be going to the New Earth. Because you are going to do it again, and again, with the same people, in the same situations, and same circumstances, until you learn to release it. And it will be worse.

If you say, I do not want to do that, you better do it now. You do not have to do it face to face. But you must do it now!

Karma simply means your actions and your responsibility. It is an internal cycle you generated.

Karma is determined only by the way you respond to what is happening to you. Karma is related to cause and effect. Karma is inevitable.

Collective karma is when you perform actions as individuals, but you can affect others as well. The suffering of collective karma can be to your family or a community.

Your destiny is what you have created for yourself. For every action you have created for yourself, there is a consequence. It always bears fruit one way or another. You make your own lives and societies positive or negative but don't try to pass it on to God. It is convenient but completely immature.

But the good news is by living consciously and fully inhabiting each moment you can free yourself from the cycle. It is possible to become ensnared by your unconscious patterns of behavior.

CHAPTER 31

Tarots Cards and the Cathars

In that early evening, I was listening to music with my eyes closed, observing my breathing, and paying attention to any sensations in my body. A rush of images appears. Epiphany or striking insights bestowed by the Divine, came to me when I least expected it. A Divine epiphany, a true gift from the spiritual realms. The very nature of unifying with higher consciousness.

The tarot cards were created by the last of the Cathars, Christians considered heretics by the Church of Rome and brutally suppressed. They were the Perfecti. The ones that want to bring people close to God.

Mysticism is a long journey, not a religion, where one becomes awakened.

I knew that no matter how painful it was, I had to endure with all the wisdom and grace I could bring forth from all, CHADD and I, years of work. We have been robbed of so many years of our lives.

But we have been called upon in this present time of chaos to show the man on Earth to remember and navigate this confusing time.

As the day went by, thousands of people died of COVID-19 while millions were protesting for social injustice around the world. But Covid was an excuse for the powerful reptilian self-elected people in key places to censor unpopular opinions.

Bricks and the nations launched a New Joint gold-backed currency to counter the US dollar dominance. Bricks Group is an association of five major emerging national economies, Brazil, India, China, and South Africa has captured the world's attention. And most people have no idea. Every currency will be backed by gold, and gold will destroy the FED.

My guardian Angel is telling me to stay strong and to continue moving forward on my journey, even though changes and obstacles. To keep a positive outlook to overcome anything.

CHAPTER 32
The Awakening and the Hopi Prophecy

My blue flame CHADD years ago kept asking "Can purity be stolen?" A revelation suddenly came to me one night. The puzzle is falling into place. That has to do with the Indian Hopy tribe and their Prophecy.

In the West, time is history, there is a past, a present, and a future. A beginning, a middle, and an end. Native people experience time as a cycle. There are four stages such as seasons: spring, summer, autumn, and winter. Like a hoop, each stage is a preparation for the next. at the center stage is preparation for the next. At the center hoop is a still timelessness, the eternal present around which the cycles revolve. The visions of native prophets occur at that center point from where the cycle of change can be seen. There is no end.

White Eagle, in his wisdom, told his son and me that when interpreting dreams or prophecies, it should be remembered that a liberal approach is misleading. Rather than the end of the world, what is implied is a transformation of consciousness from one view of the world to another and the emergence of a new world. Referred to as Ascension and the Fifth Dimension.

For years, the shamans had prophesied the end of the Earth cycle, the disappearance of the white man, and the return of all living things that vanished under the pressures of the world. He told us the time was near; even his Indian brothers, the Mayans, had predictions of a new world order that existed for many seasons. He said only by honoring Mother Earth can we avert disaster.

White Eagle told us to always remember that the scientist and explorer in us function out of the consciousness and our hearts (reconnection to the heart) To not only use our minds but our hearts to guide us in the night. That one day there will be a change of worlds, and we must use everything that we possess to cross the threshold into a new earth.

White Eagle also told me about the myth that Christ came from white man first and he was killed for his trouble. The Messiah said he would return, and he had. He was known to the Indians as Messiah, the Waneka "One who makes life", the Christ, as many believed, was called Wavoka.

He heard a voice, which commanded him to travel to the south where rivers run deep. He followed the voice to the village of Wavoka, where hundreds of other pilgrims of different tribes were. All came to meet the Messiah.

"I have sent for you and I am glad to see you," Wavoka said. "I am going to talk to you about your relatives that are dead and gone. My children, I want you to listen to all I have to say to you." Wavoka spoke to his believers. He told them that there was another world coming just like a cloud. It would come in a whirlwind of the west and would crush everything on this world." which was old and dying and those are peace in their hearts already are in the great shelter of life. That there is no shelter for evil. In that world, there was plenty of meat, just like old times, and in that world, all the dead Indians were alive, and all the bison that had been killed were roaming again." Wavoka also said, the war will bring on the new world will be a conflict with material matters. Material matters will be destroyed by spiritual beings who will remain to create one world and one nation under the power of the Creator. That time is not far off."

Isn't it about the destruction of the Elite that elected themselves to govern and enslave human beings? Isn't it about the end of the actual banking system? Are we not talking here about NEASARA/GESARA?

So, the White Eagle gave Wavoka directions to access a place where he could climb the mountaintops and live among the animals and eventually return to his father, the Great Spirit. When they had reached the plains Wavoka told him "I will leave my word in a black cave that sparkles in the mountains to bring light into the world. Whoever finds it will know it is a gift, and they must share it with others. Only when the time is right and with the right person will my world be with you and the others of the morning sun always."

The Hopi Indian prophecy states, "When the blue star Kashina makes its appearance in the heavens, the Fifth World will emerge" This will be the day of purification.

Blue star Kashina is a Kashina, a spirit, signifying the coming of the new world by appearing in the form of a blue star, and our reality is a bipolar electromagnetic energy grid program. Blue is the color of electricity. Hum! Wow! The Hopi name for the star Sirius is blue star Kashina.

The Hopi people have warned us that the world is headed for an extension. It is a Hopi prophecy revelation about the coming end of civilization on Earth.

And came to appear one huge flash shooting up a blue light over the Russian country. A pulsating blue light battered the city in southern Russia. It was a dazzling burst of light that seemed to knock out some streetlamps in the city. A celestial phenomenon combined with many military drills, the confrontation with west Ukraine, the bursting of one of Moscow's major Monasteries, and the mysterious disappearance of the Russian president for 10 days. The first encounter with the president and some E.T.

Ukraine is a hub for human and specifically child trafficking. It is a center point for narcotics weapons trafficking, bio labs (developing biological weapons), and money laundering.

The blue star Kashina, the prophecy of the Hopi will mark down the end of an old and the beginning of a new world and within days the world was knocked down because of Covid.

Blue Star Kashina is a Kashina or a spirit, signifying the beginning of a New World by appearing in the form of a blue star. The Hopi people have warned us the world is headed for extinction.

We are in a Cosmic War. You must repent, repent, repent, and be consecrated to the Immaculate Heart of Mary.

Elites try to erase MT/DNA mitochondria, steal innocence, split the Soul, and take the Soul of children with the body. They can recognize who people are by looking at the genetics of people through a looking glass.

It is a Hopi prophecy revelation about the coming end of civilization on Earth. The Indian prophecy States, "When the blue star makes its appearance in the heavens, the Fifth world will emerge" This all be the day of purification.

CHAPTER 33

Welcome to the Digital Battlefield

Many of my clients bring pages of their dreams to the session, wanting an explanation. Dreams are messages, If the subconscious has tried to get a message across in many different ways, and the person does not understand, it will deliver it another way.

I suddenly felt a high-frequency vibration and heard, "Hey! VIE, it's me, said the Messenger. I have been sent to you, and I want to share one message with you. It is a time when the old is breaking down, and the new is coming in. The self-elected and their Satanists' minions Hybrids have a plan. The project Sky Blue Technology.

They plan to create some holographic Spacecraft in all major cities and make them look like Aliens attacking the planet. Their ultimate goal is to establish the New World Order, so that humanity may come together against these intergalactic pirates.

These "parasites" have already been working on flying aircrafts, and directed energy weapons, so fooling the masses into another poorly directed Hollywood movie will not be too difficult.

But they have lost, and they know it! The truth is the military has everything to expose them and does not need the election audit results. Exposure is coming.

I want to talk a little bit about what is happening and some of the reasons why it is happening. On Planet Earth, there are many different factions, and they are all fighting for their own version of reality. They are fighting for their own version of control, and they don't want other people to have power and freedom. So, there have been struggles for control of the world for many thousands of years.

This has been a very violent planet because of the degree of separation that exists among human beings, and all other life forms on the planet. The separation between humanity as a collective and the planet itself. This separation exists because of the energy that has been used by those who have controlled you. The energy that has come from rage, hatred, anger, and fear.

Frequently you see these energies expressed in physical ways, through pandemics, war, or over political power. These things occur because the old energy patterns are still playing out on your planet

There is a lot of change happening in this process of the old breaking down on your planet right now. Many people are feeling fear, confusion, and a sense of loss as they try to make sense of the world around them. While it is true that there is a feeling of chaos in the world today, many positive changes are occurring at the same time as these chaotic ones.

It is becoming apparent that in your physical world, the old systems are failing, and they are failing rapidly. The food systems are failing. the educational system is not preparing for what you need to know to be successful in life. The energy systems are not allowing you to move forward with the technologies available to you today.

As you know, the old financial system has broken down and is undergoing massive change. Old systems in governments and other organizations are being replaced with new, more equitable ones. The energy on your planet is allowing all this to occur so that your society can evolve into one that is more loving, fair, and compassionate.

People from countries that were once at odds with each other are becoming allies to avert a major war. This breakup of old alliances will allow for greater peace on your planet in the future.

The new financial system is being implemented very slowly because there are still those who would prefer to hold onto the old ways of doing things. The new way of doing business will be based on equality rather than greed, so it requires some time for people to adjust their thinking and behavior.

You may have many dreams about the future and a new life for yourself, and you may feel the excitement building within you because you know that a change is coming. And yes it is!

You are all creating this change because you are all co-creators. You have put it into motion through your thoughts and your feelings because your feelings create reality. You have put this change out into the universe, and now it is coming back to you. It may not come in exactly the way that you expect it to come or at exactly the time that you expect it to come but be assured that it is coming. It has been birthed by your thoughts and desires, and now it is manifesting for you.

There will be much upheaval on Earth in the next few months as old systems break down and new systems are born. Change is coming to every country, every city, every town, and every village.

Some things are changing faster than others, but the changes are happening all over the planet. This is such an exciting time to be alive on Earth. There is so much change happening in every different aspect of life as well as in your individual lives. Some of you may be experiencing more change than others, depending on your journey. But no matter what is going on for you in your life, know that the universe is working with you and for you in every area. It has your back, and it's always there, ready to help. Just ask, that's all it takes!

A new paradigm is emerging with a new financial system that is based on truth and love, not debt and control. These changes will affect everyone on the planet. It's time to let go of the old way of doing things so you can create your own future. Creating your future starts with letting go of the past.

Let go of the past, it is time to let go of fear and negative emotions so you can create your future. Fear is an illusion created to keep you from creating what you want in your life. You are loved and wanted on this planet! You have gifts that others need. You have a purpose in life that is unique only to you! If you're feeling overwhelmed, it's time to let go of the past, forgive yourself, forgive others, and start fresh today! You made this choice at some point in your life, or even lifetimes ago, and it is now becoming more apparent as the time of transition upon your planet accelerates!

The New Earth is already here! It has been here for a long time! It is now becoming more visible to those who choose to see it. Those who choose to remain in the old consciousness, the old-world order, will remain blind to this process of ascension and will continue their path of destruction and separation from their creator".

CHAPTER 34

When my Star Sister appears to Speak of NESARA/GESARA

The Pleiadians are aware of the danger on planet Earth. I was sitting at my desk when my star sister appeared to me and said:

"Hello, VIE, it is me your star sister. I know that you have heard of NESARA (the National Economic Stabilization and Recovery Act) written in the 1970s?" she said.

But many have not. Most of those who have heard about it are confused. They confuse it with the mark of the beast. But it has nothing to do with the Mark of the Beast.

A new financial system will be and is being released into the world to pull the world away from the Fiat currency into a Gold-Backed currency that will bring about freedom and a lack of Debt. But too many have read Revelation, and they believe, mistakenly, that NESARA and GESARA are the Mark.

GESARA: Global Economic Security and Reform Act
NESARA: National Economic Security and Recovery Act:

1. NESARA/GESARA: cancels all credit cards, mortgages, and other bank debt due to illegal banking and Government activities refer to this as "jubilee" or complete forgiveness of debt

2. Abolishes income tax
3. Abolishes the IRS
4. Creates a 17% flat rate for non-essential new items, only sales tax revenue for the government. Food and medicine are not taxed; nor used items as old homes.
5. Increases benefits for senior citizens
6. Returns Constitutional Law to all courts and legal matters.
7. Reinstates the original title of Nobility Amendment
8. Establishes New Presidential and Congressional elections within 120 days of GESARA. The interim Government will cancel all National Emergencies and return us to constitutional law
9. Monitors elections and prevents illegal election activities of special interest groups
10. Creates a new U.S. Treasury rainbow currency backed by gold, silver, and platinum   precious metals, ending the bankruptcy of the United States initiated by Franklin Roosevelt in 1933
11. Forbids the sale of American birth certificate records as chattel property bonds by the US Department of Transportation
12. Initiates new US Treasury Bank System in alignment with Constitutional Law
13. Eliminating the Federal Reserve System (FED) during the transition period the Federal Reserve System will be allowed to operate side by side of the US Treasury for one year in order to remove notes from the money supply.
14. Restores Financial privacy
15. Restrains all judges and attorneys in Constitutional Law

16. Ceases all aggressive, US Government military actions worldwide
17. Establish peace throughout the world
18. Restores unprecedented prosperity with emotional sums of money for humanitarian purposes
19. Enables release of over 6,000 patents suppressed technologies that are being withheld from the public under the guise of National Security, including free energy devices, anti-gravity, and sonic machines
20. Eliminate all current and future nuclear-powered weaponry on planet Earth.

This is what is definitively coming.

CHAPTER 35
The Benei Elohim, the Origins of Evil, and the Adrenochrome

I tried to recall. The memory has never changed, I remember and it's vivid. One world is a conspiracy, and the transgender agenda originates from the Elohim. Most churches have lost their way and brainwashed people, and my task is not easy.

But my ancestor Hughes Capet came to my help and said to me. As you may recall the Capetians founded a dynasty, affirming the politician's independence from the King of England and the Pope. Our ancestors were Catholic though and this period gave birth to eight years of crusades and Christianity began to change.

Then the humanitarian foundation created by Jesus eroded as Christianity became more political. And you see, said Hughes, the Nephilim are Alien and the story of divine beings procreating with a human woman brought sin to humanity, causing the ancient flood as well, and this sin to humanity, causing the ancient flood as well, and this sin is the source of disease in the present day. Nephilim is a giant race of alien-human hybrids.

"Genesis 2 That the sons of God saw the daughters of men that they were fair; and they took them wives of all which they chose."

In the Book of Enoch, the watchers are angels sent to Earth to watch over the Humans. But they soon begin to lust for human women and, at the prodding of their leader Samyaza, defect to illicitly instruct Humanity and procreate among them.

The first part of the Book of Enoch describes the fall of the Watchers, the angels who fathered the angel-human hybrids called Nephilim. "Gen 6-5 And YHWH saw the wickedness of man was great on the Earth, and that inclination of thoughts of his heart was only evil continually."

"Gen 6-6 And YHWH regretted that He has made man on earth, and it grieved his heart." So they took a human woman who became pregnant and bore large giants. These devoured all the toil of men until they were not able to sustain them. And the giants turned against them in order to devour the man. Then they began to sin against birds, animals, reptiles, and fish, and they devoured one another's flesh and drank the blood from it. Then the Earth complained about lawless ones.

Now that the earth is moving into the Fifth Dimension, some humans are beginning to awaken, open their eyes, and see it. Even though the media are trying to hide it. It is led by the government of the world that is self-elected in key places. With their created pandemic, a "Plandemy" part of their agenda is to not only kill humans (part of the population's reduction), with the Covid vaccination, but also the pharmaceutical drugs that make men infertile. They are trying to keep humans unawakened to better control them. They traffic humans, kidnap kids to rape them, torture them, kill them, eat their flesh, and drink their blood, they sell and call adrenochrome. The elitists tortured kidnapped children and extracted their blood. And the cartel was kidnapped to empty the body of its organs for resale and fill up the body with drugs.

God is not behind human disease or the human inclination to sin. Instead, it is the evil on spirits that are themselves the result of an angelic transgression against God's will.

But at the end when God commands Archangel Michael all earth will be cleansed of evil and wickedness, all peoples will worship God, and everyone will live in peace for eternity (*1 Enoch* 10:21-11:2):

CHAPTER 36
When Satan revealed himself in PEP-SEE and the Russians Were fighting the Khazarian Mafia in their Homeland.

On an early fall morning, I looked out the window pensively trying to remember, and each time I remembered I got a smell attached to it. I look at the large clock on the wall. I think imagination is creation. Then, I am humbled by the knowledge pouring into me. I went back to my nocturnal dream. The beautiful white light occupies my field.

But have in vision the world that is a conspiracy.

A favorite Hockey player drinks Pepsi as I see. Satan revealed itself in the favorite Hockey player Pepsi. I am entering a building with big gold doors, and a black marble floor with a large crystal in the center. A woman touches the crystal, and it activates. The crystal sets a resonance that allows the knowledge to be downloaded and received. The woman is a communicator and brings up a point. She says she is here to bring the knowledge. The word Pepsi comes from Apep, the Egyptian God of evil, darkness, and destruction. The word Pepsi means PEP-SEE. The eye of Apep is the logo. That's a serpent eye of Apep. The ancient Egyptians were practicing Satanists whose rites included child sacrifice and cannibalism. The logo is the serpent eye of the reptilians, the controllers on Earth. Graphene Oxide has now been confirmed to be found in vax vials, in masks, in swabs and now in hand sanitizer.

A Reach American computer programmer businessman wants to block out the sun to change the climate by dispersing nanoparticles into the stratosphere. The same process is seen in the sky with chemtrails. After a couple of hours of spraying, the weather turns from sunny to cloudy. It looks grayish, cloudy layer that gets stuck there, it neither rains nor gets more or less cloudy. And you breathe it.

In 1960 twenty generals began the fight against the Khazarian mafia who created the slave trade and owned 99% of the US slaves. Today the battle is coming to an end.

Years ago, I predicted the end of the pharmaceutical pills as we know it now. I told you that we will transition from crystalline-based DNA, and we will become immortal. I told you that CHADD and I, the God Duo, were bringing you oneness. Does not matter what they try to make you think it would be.

The Old Earth. as I write, it is still under the rule of darkness, but we will soon enter the new. During the transition, carbon-based bodies will be replaced by crystalline-based light bodies. These Light bodies are real physical manifestations of the new crystalline network that is gradually appearing within the new Earth's collective consciousness field. They are not ethereal or astral. They exist in physical form. They exist in these physical forms as the current bodies do, but they are composed of a more refined matter-energy matrix and are more finely tuned to the resonant frequency of your true self, your multidimensional, eternal essence that exists beyond time and space.

There is no death on the New Earth. It will be a paradise place. It will be replaced by Oneness. The new

Earth has been created by God Almighty, you will be transfigured to the New Earth through Ascension.

I entered the scene. We are all going into this meeting room. I think they are going to tell us something. A man is doing the talking. I believe he is a warrior. He has a sword on him. It looks like it's a military takeover. The people wear clothes, there is no differentiation, no status between anyone else.

Now my awareness is expanding. Sound is important and there is a light scent. I am following the sound of music and vibration, and I am floating on the vibration. I let it come in. I am breathing the vibration, and I become the vibration. And there are no boundaries or barriers. I am riding the vibration.

I am taught by it. I learned everything from it, it is vibrating rate. I can live on the Light and it can be food. I do not need to eat anything else unless I choose to.

I am here to do something important. There are dangers to observe. There is some kind of purpose to all that. It's for my purpose. I have a big piece of paper, and a writing pen, and we are figuring it all out. I have to be part of that, and we are talking about that. I felt light and could see muted colors.

It is like a curtain, a white veil opening. Now I understand. I have learned two things. How to defeat the dark agenda with my vibration.

I am attending a convention, I am exposing my books and giving a lecture. A man stands next to my booth. He stays there first and stares at me. Not a blink of his eyes. Then he approaches the table and touches the books. I do not feel comfortable and wait for him to leave. But he went back to where he was, standing there looking towards me and the table. I realized he was standing in the way of the people approaching and looking at my books. The man finally moves out of the way. I am living by myself. I am going to the conference room where I am expected to give a speech. The man is not far standing at the entrance of the conference room. I look at the clock and someone is still occupying the room, though it is my time. After a few minutes, I get upset, my vibrations are high at that point, and I hear myself saying loud in an angry voice "Oh! No! That's enough. Enough is enough. My audience is waiting for me." And I saw the man, who was previously on the way next to my booth, leaving. It took the door running as fast as he could. And we never saw him again."

That is when the warrior man said: High vibration scares the dark spirit. He could not stand your elevated vibration. They cannot stay with high vibration. Remember you carry a high transformative Energy. It heals on every level. That is how you defeat the controllers and bit their agenda.

For the Russians, they are fighting the Khazarian mafia in their homeland. They are cutting the head off the snake of the group that has been destroying the planet for generations. Because they control this country like they control everywhere else. And the Russians along with many other nations and many other militaries are actually fighting a subterranean war to exterminate vermin from the planet. I am the "warrior man" part of the Army special forces.

The second thing I learned about was the CERN. It is a Large Hadron Collider. A particle accelerator to recreate, they say, black holes, antimatter and rip holes with the same time continuum opening up dimensional portals.

In fact, CERN deals with subatomic dimensions. It is radio nuclear research Physicists doing very strange experiments. From the bottom of the CERN, beings are coming in and out from the portals. Portals are doors to another dimension. Some researchers say there are seventeen dimensions and others say there are even more. There is a fight with some military agencies. They are trying to change the time. And I thought no wonder the planet is in turbulence.

CHAPTER 37
A Vision of the Truth Worldwide

I saw all the material things in my room disappearing, it was just a matter of an instant. I was contemplating supernatural matters. But I heard a great deal about the matter. I traveled to a lot of places. It is what explains everything that we see happening today. As darkness falls every lie gets revealed.

The blood of millions of lives over the decades lies in the hands of the most public serial killer. In 1962 recommended vaccine schedule for US Children was only Polio, Smallpox and DTP. Since 2019 from birth to 12 years old children are required to receive 32 vaccinations. Without counting the 2 (influenza and TDaP) during pregnancy.

The so-called "pandemic" was planned and globally coordinated decades in advance. A newly resurfaced interview from some years ago of an Elite said, "It's been proven that when you make it difficult for people in their lives they lose their ideological nonsense and get vaccinated". Four deadly parasites have been found in vaccines. Hydra Vulgaris (Moderna), Trypanosoma Cruzi (Pfizer) T. Brucei (Pfizer), Polypodium Hydriform (Moderna). Meanwhile, the fully vaccinated continue to dominate infection, hospitalization, and mortality rates.

There is a video from the 90s on mind control via microwave EMF and the Tele-lies-vision. In a shocking secret presentation to central intelligence, an influential billionaire talks about different parts of the brain and how it can be controlled with drugs and vaccines.

Our mobile phones have become the greatest spy on the planet. HAARP changes the Earth's frequencies to create earthquakes. Popular sweetener aspartame causes anxiety by changing brain structure and setting up mental disorders such as anxiety. These changes persist for up to 2 subsequent generations.

A geologist said, "Governments need a crisis with which to frighten people, to control them more effectively, which is why only scientists who push the fraudulent human-indued climate crisis narrative receive any funding." Wow Isn't a government gone insane?

The voting process is an illusion and a government that fluctuates between two extremes. It's political. Each extreme annulling any progress made by the opposition in the prior administration.

Some actors and musicians try to deny selling their souls to the controllers of the planet to become famous. A musician admits to selling his soul for fame and understands the consequences of what he did in front of a cameraman who interview him. But regrets what he did. He made a bargain with the devil and does not know he sang some songs. He has no idea where the lyrics come from.

In psychiatric units we are not dealing with these Thuggees Psychopaths anymore but with these Non-Human Satanists. They look through a looking glass and can recognize our genetics. It is just a takeaway of human DNA and Souls and builds something to hold up us. They thought we would never wake up and now it scares them.

Chemo is microwaving a Pathologist said. All patients dead of cancer never died of cancer. Their organs have been cooked.

CHAPTER 38

Then I received this message from Sananda

I went to have a quick bite before my appointment for a facial and my attention was attracted by a black couple entering with a baby. The mother was carrying a gorgeous and perfect baby in her arms. The baby was blond with curly hair and beautiful blue eyes. But something was weird, there were no signs of life in the eyes. That was my first encounter with a baby clone. This disturbed me a lot all day. I kept thinking about it all day.

The night came and I went to bed. I had a little bit of difficulty falling asleep still thinking about this so beautiful though baby.

That is when I received this message:

Do clones exist? Who can be saved? and can every soul be saved?

Not every soul can be saved. Because it requires being willing to leave the path they have chosen and turn around. There are souls that are completely surrendered to the destructive despot. These souls are being restructured, being brought back to unity. In due time they will have a new opportunity to experiment with themselves as human beings. They start a new cycle of incarnation by entering a lower level of consciousness.

This Earth is populated by human clones without a soul. On the outside, they are in no way different from humans, so they are difficult to recognize. However, for those who can see through the subtlety, this distinction can be seen clearly. d artificially and have no purpose; to lead people astray from their divine path.

Clones have no aura. they emit a cold electromagnetic field that produces no color. this cold white light is the signature of signature. they are creating.

Many designers and leaders have nothing human in them. It's easy for them to act inhumanly, injustice and arbitrariness tempt inspired people to abandon the path of Light. They develop foreign fears to a sane person, fears that they feed on the principles of darkness, Human clones were the collectors of the energies of fear.

The new Erath is populated by people with a soul. Only those who dwell inwardly will find a place here because the New Earth is a place of vibrancy, sincerity, and love.

The kingdom of peace on Earth requires another human being willing to heal themselves in divine light and who has a real desire for unity and knowledge.

Your ascension means the descent of those who have used the wheel of time to their favor without tending to the souls of men. This game is over.

Life will triumph and there will be Light on this Earth. The forces that have so far controlled this infiltration process are diminishing. The dark princes must leave the Earth and die with them including those who served them and gave them a helping hand.

CHAPTER 39

A Spirit standing at my footbed and some shocking revelations

This revelation happened while I was sleeping soundly in my bed. Around 3 o'clock, my eyes snapped open, and I caught sight of a spirit standing at the foot of my bed, staring at me. I think he is a warrior. He has a sword on him. He is sending me images and visions telepathically.

It's a military takeover. The clothes the people wear are all the same. There is no differentiation, no status between anyone.

My awareness is expanding. Now there is a scent and a sound. Sound is important. Portals are opened through sound frequencies. When two cords resonate in octaves they create a phantom beat or resonant energy that can open portals.

This is how the pyramid would function. Dispersing a frequency into the ionic sphere, using monoatomic gold as a conductor as a smart dust to transfer the information at the speed of Light.

The Great Pyramid of Giza emits a frequency of 432 Hz. Other pyramids have different frequencies. They are set on lay lines. If they started to resonate, it would activate the chakras. The crystalline body. And because the pyramids are aligned to the constellations, everyone would sing in harmony with the Universe.

Following the sounds of the music and vibration I become the sound. I am breathing the vibration and I become the vibration. There are no boundaries or barriers. I ride the vibration. I am taught by it. I learn everything from it. The sound is vibrating, and I can live on the light, it becomes food. I do not need to eat anything else than light unless I choose to.

I chose to come here to help you. Everything I offer you is meant to be as medicine to nourish your Mind and to expand your horizon. Everything you see or hear is not like it looks like. There are dangers to observing but there is a purpose to all that.

I have a pen and some paper. A big piece of paper and a pen to write, and we are all together figuring it out. I must be a part of that, and we are talking about it.

I felt the Light and could see muted colors. It is like a veil opening. Poisons are being sprayed daily in the skies, and there is nobody doing anything about it don't wait for disaster to strike. Government secrets are hard to achieve, but when exposed can be jaw-dropping and could be the center of a political storm.

Some Royal family tries to silence and assassinate a Princess, but she is alive. The cabal tried to do the same with the son of a President, but he is alive The Elites tried to silence and assassinate a very famous musician and failed. There are the innocent victims who will make the world better. And there will come a time when they will be able to walk down the street without fear. The true spirit of victory and change is coming though. Get ready!

Now I understand. We have learned how to beat the dark agenda with Vibration, light, scent, and colors. Nothing is fixed and everything can be changed.

Just expand your horizon, and realize you are the co-creator in power. Get above the third-dimension thinking. Get over the programming. Stop making your obstruction. You are powerful and they fear it. Use your instinct as your GPS and follow it. Thrive to do it as long as it feels good. You will then change your perception and ride a higher view and just make it happen. You will beat the dark agenda.

Good! Because we are living in a holographic Game. The game was set up years ago by the Freemasons with different rules. There is the Bible for Christians, the Torah for the Jews, and the Quran for the Muslims.

This is already the start of the division among humans living on Earth. It's dividing to control better. Then the Freemasons, the elite, and their minions create fights for the richest in countries and for the power to govern each. Wars create more benefits and more money. So, they create battles for resources, like oil, gold, nickel, uranium, diamonds…And wars also serve their agenda. It reduces the population and is an opportunity for genocide.

Thank you for the information I said. Then he disappeared.

CHAPTER 40

The Re-Call

The majority of Souls on Earth are trapped in the cycle until they complete it.

Agnes a friend of my neighbor was going through a simple, mundane primitive life when she was invited to look at a movie that shook her badly. Violent as she described it. Agnes went home and straight to bed. In the middle of the night, she heard a voice saying:

"I ask you to move ahead while something important is happening."

Agnes was shaking with fear when she started remembering the violent scene in the movie she saw earlier. All she recalled was the violence, to go hide in one of the suggested safe places, and the president was killed at the end. and the movie Agnes went to see, is played in movie theatres just before an important election time. I will understand a few months later why she was so disturbed by the movie. She understood humanity was awakening and powerful.

The movie shows two journalists sharing some personal information about two photos' shootings. They share their disagreement with both families living a normal life on a farm and pretending nothing was happening in the world. While there was a war going on.

Then comes a scene that one actor describes as a "twilight zone". When the journalists cannot believe what they are seeing passing through a small town. They entered a small boutique. The vendor welcomes them without lifting her head from the book she is reading. One journalist asks the vendor if she is aware of what is happening out there at that time. The vendor finally lifted her head and replied "Yes, of course! But… Hey! Life continues." She told them to try whatever they would like to, and she got back to her reading.

The movie suggests educating oneself and searching for the truth. Not hiding on a farm, a barn, or a small community. It shows some scenes of genocide, and many bodies were killed and discharged in a big hole in the dirt. Like history repeating itself. The Holocaust.

But people are so indoctrinated and programmed. Because of the amnesia at birth. The problem on Earth is too many souls are caught and trapped in the cycle of death and rebirth which unfortunately serve the controllers.

The movie can be seen positively or negatively. It all depends on where you stand on your journey. The movie suggests a president is killed at the end and suggests some safe places to hide in case of war. Please remember that you are the co-creator, the Elite in power can't create without you, but they can use humans and propel the brain this way to make it happen. It's the only way it can happen. Never without your consent.

You can manifest whatever you want. A whistleblower, former intelligence officer, and author speak and explain. Israel was created as the instrument to bring about a war that would be terrible, where nuclear weapons would be used so that people would get down on their knees and beg for no more wars. And the answer to that is that the controllers are going reply and say, "The only way we can guarantee no more war is if we destroy the sovereignty of nations and we come together as one humanity in a one world government."

At the ascension the rainbow colors will appear in the sky, rain will stop, it's the solar flash prophecy. The sun will come down toward the earth and the just will be transformed (Ascension) and the wicked will be consumed by it. The dark spirits plan to be gone before it happens.

CHAPTER 41

The Quantum Dot, The Hydrogel and the Hydrogel Mask

Time has never been so crucial and CHADD & VIE have to go through many more tribulations to free humanity. They are battling the enemies without ceasing. The angels' Cosmic couple returned at a crucial time on Earth.

Because you are at a pivotal moment of change, and the trust and belief the Cosmic couple share with you have never been more important.

The Elite in power, the controllers want all humans eradicated. Their first step is to increase the human population from 8 billion to one. A Prominent Club of Rome member, hopes the necessary depopulation of planet Earth, down to one billion, is an 87,5 percent reduction of the population and it "can occur in a civil war."

They chip the brain, inject hydrosol particles in vaccinations and continue to kill by creating diseases, air pollution, poisoning food and drinks…

With the corona PCR tests. A scientist immunologist and virologist said the CDC was a massive fraud. From 1500 samples of people who tested "positive" all people were simply found to have influenza A to a lesser extent influenza B.

They also are implanting microchips. Not only do people's bodies biologically change but it is the tag. All are owned and operated by Rockefeller. This is part of the barcode initiated to take and identify all life forces. All life force. The COVID situation was the first deployment of a construct of a new life form and allowed the use of a biological of life in Robotics. The purpose is for extermination. They do not want anything of the old world. They want a new world and very soon. Their goal is to have all humans eradicated and from now on all be engineered in a laboratory and part of the matrix. They want to rewire your body. Each human right now has twenty thousand to thirty thousand nanoparticles.

The controllers wanted to insert chips in people's brains but didn't want to have to do surgery and they came with a gel. It's called hydrogel, or Quantum dot. What happens with the vaccine you get injected, is that it then assembles, then swings before crossing your blood-brain barrier and it takes over your brain. It then harvests the fluid in your body moisture and grows and grows, and humans are no longer humans. The biological cells die because there is nothing left.

The only way to avoid it is to refuse and say No to COVID tests, and vaccinations.

There is also a hydrogen mask where you breathe every breath you take; you are breathing in these hydrogel particles. These elite worshippers of Satan deploy all these nano symbionts into the body, and they can carry poison. The hydrogel mask is a tool that gets its marching orders from the frequency that has been inhaled, and it is bio-accumulative. The more you get of it, it stays in your body and it will not go out.

People on Earth, you are living in a new era and if human beings want to ascend, they better hurry, you better hurry to be more preoccupied with researching and understanding the truth hidden to you by the cabal.

Thirteen years ago, a politician said that once the herd accepts mandatory vaccinations, it's game over. They will accept anything forcible, blood or organ donation for "the greater good". We can genetically modify and sterilize them for "The greater good", control the sheep's minds and you control the herd. Vaccine makers stand to make billions, and it is a big win-win for investors.

It is a question of being your power, or somebody else, a being in control of an organization. They are about the source consciousness.

Now, let's embark on a journey to discover the mystery of the Quantum you. Much like the particles, your lives are filled with potential and shaped by your thoughts and beliefs. Just as a particle settles into a specific state when observing life, your life takes shape based on how you see the world. Your thoughts are the creator of your reality. What you believe influences what you experience. If your beliefs are narrow, so are your possibilities. But when you open yourself up to the vast potential of your mind, you will see your life transform in ways you never thought was possible

Because nothing is set in stone, and the realm of possibility stretches out endlessly until you decide otherwise. Your thoughts don't just shape your reality, figuratively but literally, on a quantum level.

Together the people are unstoppable. Together you are the bearers of the Light of freedom, illuminating the path forward. Step bravely into the dawn of this revolution.

Trust the plan, the best is to come. You are offered a chance to join the rest of the universe in peace and participate in spiritual awakening. Something the controllers Elite wouldn't like to see happening.

Pain is coming. Soon you will understand who they awakened and provoked and they will not like it.

CHAPTER 42
Digital Army, Global Military Alliance, Global Alliance

I woke up that morning with my left eye vision blurry and remembered clearly years ago the eye specialist Mrs. Spencer telling me never to let anyone tell me that I have a cataract. You will never have cataracts.

My left eye is the window of the heart, and the light of the heart goes through and to the left eye. Like the right eye is connected to our etheric field.

The blurry vision in my left eye makes me understand I have to stay invisible in the dark. So, I put myself invisible to the dark.

And Now I decided to call the light beings of the sixth and said, "Glorious and powerful sixth-dimensional level light beings, open up a portal between the sixth dimension and us the God duo, where we are stuck now and then we transition up the portal and under the sixth dimension, we become firmly established there."

Confirmation came right away. We had to transition up the portal. The phone rang it was a client calling for information. The law of attraction is a brainwave. It's a possibility where everything exists.

Let's continue the journey to discover the mystery of the quantum you. This evolution results in humanity regaining its wings from the great fall. Somewhere deep within you know something is happening that you can't quite see. Tiny synchronicities align in perfect timing.

The digital Army is the largest fighting force ever mustered, dismantling an ancient multi-million dollar, "consciousness, control weapon of war" at a speed never possible before.

A global military alliance is underway. Global Alliance has received the green light to take over major fake news media and make mass arrests.

You see we embarked on this journey years ago with you, for you. There is so much that has been hidden from you, but you have to awaken now.

In 2009 a very well-known politician said that once the Herd accepts mandatory vaccinations, it's game over. They will accept anything forcible blood or organ donation for the greater good. We can genetically modify children and sterilize them "for the greater good". Control sheep minds and you control the herd vaccine makers stand to make billions. And for many investors, it's a win-win. It's a question of being your power to somebody else or being in control of an external organization.

The law of attraction in brainwave is a fascinating dance between your mind and the fabric of reality.

CHAPTER 43

Let the LIGHT Guide You

I went that Sunday in July to attend mass in a beautiful basilica. I needed clarity. I knew I was attacked for a few days, and I knew it was depriving me of lucidity. I could feel the turmoil. After praying for the rosary all night and requesting help from Saint Benedict I was guided by Zacharias to go to mass at this basilica dedicated to our Blessed Mother Mary Queen of the Universe. The smell when I entered the place centered me immediately. I sat next to a magnificent statue of Mary. After ten to fifteen minutes, I saw a man in his twenties coming towards me. He had dark hair and was wearing a cap and a red T-shirt. He was mumbling and I saw he was also doing some gestures. I recognized one. He was clearing something. Then the mass began, and I forgot totally about him. I noticed that the priests incensed the church and the people more than usual. When the mass ended the man was gone and nowhere to be found. That is when I realized my prayer for help had been answered. Zacharias knew this man was sent and would meet me at Church, so he made sure I would be at Church. Then I began to regain clarity of thoughts and peace entered me again. It was one of these attacks again.

As you navigate the journey into the depths of consciousness, a journey that transcends time and space, imagine if you wake up one day to find the world around you subtly differently as if seen through a new lens of perception. A sign of a profound shift taking place within you. In a time when the old ways are giving way to the new. When the familiar is morphing into the extraordinary, sometimes you cannot tell the truth to people. You must show them.

Are you ready to embrace the sign that speaks to your soul, to discover the truth that lies beyond the veil of ordinary perception? The transition from 3D to 5D life will open a higher state of being. 3D is characterized by separation, fear, and initiation. While the 5D dimension vibrates at a frequency of love.

It was night time and I was sleeping, with what I saw in my vision I became very distressed. It was very upsetting looking at what was happening on my island. It was the Civil War. All because the elite took control of the people and the media, and used their voices to make it look like they were winning. This did not have to happen. The entire population aspires the same. Peace. But it was a fight for the richness contained in the island. So what they did was they picked up a few of the minorities on the island and used them to divide the population. They convinced the oldest to drug their children and to send them burn and destroy. Their target was the economy. Destroying the administration buildings, schools, Pharmacies, Public and personal transportation, Grocery stores, and Dialysis centers, Blocking entrances of Hospitals, anHd all access to important locations in town by building barricades. They stole liquor and drank it while keeping barricades. What was even more dangerous was that they were armed and drugged by an inference of a foreign country.

It began exactly forty years ago when the dark initiated their agenda 21. These beings are from another planet full of greed and hatred. They built an alliance with a man who later on would pretend to be a native of this beautiful island. A strategic geographical place is rich in Uranium, Gold, and Nickel. Manganese, Cobalt, and much more. A peaceful jewel. A gem surrounded by turquoise water and a big lagoon. A place convoluted by a communist country mainly Muslims and by some other terrorist countries.

This failed coup attempt by overwhelmed leaders is a sad story speaking of heroes and dead people, written by a journalist. A policewoman suspected of leaking secret information to the destructors by her companion, a Security police assistant adjoint. Her companion forgot his cellphone that was revealing the trajectory of the President of the country, all phone calls made to the office of her father, the traitor to the country, and a political party manager.

It was on the following July Saturday morning, when coming back home and getting off my car there was, at my feet, a beautiful white feather. I immediately understood the Holy Spirit was with me.

Waking up on Sunday morning I drove two hours and a half from home to visit the Abbey of St Leo. I wanted to be with the Benedictine Monks during their daily mass at noon. It is a community of Benedictine monks. Constantly in prayer on behalf of the Church, working to convert their lives in service to God and each other.

On the left side of the altar is a statue of Mother Mary and a few seats next to it. I lit a candle put some money on the trunk to pay for the candle and sat in one of the seats.

I began to talk to Our Blessed Mother. As I was praying and talking to Our Blessed Lady she entered my heart. What a comfort!

There I was guided, the same way I was at the Cathedral in France. The father wanted me to speak the language of the Light and change the energy inside.

I came home excited and shared on the phone the event with my friend the astrologist, and he replied "I may think mysterious, but Our Lady is helping me now at this event time. Prayers are also directed to immediate peace to the Island."

I was so grateful and excited. Here again, the Father, Mother Mary, and the Holy Spirit were with me, guiding me, talking to me, and letting me know I was not alone.

The power of the good is the winner. Some famous people are said to be dead gone global and helped finish the holographic world and the Elites. They are accused and laughed out but whether we realize it or not, we will be shifting to another conscious world. The island is protected.

I have been led to see that at any time now a turn of events will trigger the unbelievable. Our entire Government will be invalidated. The storm has arrived and has information to bring the whole illegitimate regime down and back to the constitutional law of the land and get rid of the law of the sea. It will bring world peace for one thousand years and eliminate all current and future nuclear weapons on the planet Earth. The power then goes back to the people with the global distribution of wealth.

Getting up the following morning I could barely stand up due to the gravity on my body. An unusual weight of gravity. Then I remembered gravity can be used to hold people down. Gravity originally was released by the Divine but dark forces use it for the wrong reason. And they were on me. But the fact I acknowledged it the weight progressively left me.

Like the so-called pandemic was planned and coordinated in advance, as part of a supranational operation to deliberately depopulate the planet using lethal mRNA injections.

CHAPTER 44

Genesis 6 and the Anti-Christ

I was going to get up and was about to open my eyes and this new vision appeared to me.

The universe is working for you, Heaven is holding a conversation, and angels have been assigned to you. It's going to be alright even though secret societies and the descendants of giants have planned to enslave humankind.

Their bloodlines extend back to the Nephilim, from the angels that mated with human women. When God cast the angels, Lucifer and his followers out of heaven. Lucifer set into motion a plan of action to ensure the Nephilim will survive. Because from the bloodlines of these Nephilim, the anti-Christ will come.

Satan enlisted the loyalty of the secret societies, the Freemasons, the templars, and the Rosecrucians to conspire to teach theology and history of the world that is contrary to the Biblical one. In Genesis 6, conspiracy marches toward the great tribulation, when the loyalty of the terminal generation, today's generation, is tested.

Nostradamus saw in his future three anti-Christ. One was Napoleon, the second was Hitler and the 3rd one that is to come. The one to come is the worst of all because he learned from the mistakes of all the others. He is very dangerous. He does terrible things to people and does not care about what he is interested in is power.

In the book of Revelation and the Old Testament, the prophets saw the same. The number 666 is called the beast. 666 refers to his connection to the computers. He has a destiny to fulfill, and he has to come. But after that, it is in the hands of mankind.

The anti-Christ is now alive. He saw that he was born February 4th, 1962, in Jerusalem, but is not Jewish. He was raised at 6 years old by his uncle. He went to college in Egypt and has study as main courses economics, philosophy, and computers. Computers will be very important in his life. It is connected to 666.

The uncle is an evil man. He killed his parents to take the boy and raise him as his own, but the anti-Christ does not know it. The uncle put a very powerful group of rich Arabs from the Middle East together to groom the anti-Christ. All in this group are puppets and they are the ones that control everything in the Middle East.

Beware, the anti-Christ will appear as the Savior. He is the wolf in sheep's clothing with a golden tongue. By the time the seven trumpets arrive, you will realize what happened.

CHAPTER 45

An Illusionary World

Years ago, I received a message.

Another vision appeared suddenly while some cult people were trying to convince me to enter their group. They pretended to be the disciples. I saw the letters of the Bible, some Bold letters in Gold. I did not understand the message at that time.

Rosecrucian and Freemasons translated the Bible, and they are controlling the world. They use symbols of pyramids, masonic eyes, crosses with roses all around, faces making the sign of silence, Indonesian idol Goddesses, by practicing Egyptian magic and spells...And no one realizes when they see it the importance it has to control human beings.

Looking at the Universe the visibility changes everything. As I look over the archives the familiar stories of the book of Genesis affirm certain things, however, various anomalies in the text clue that we are not reading the original version of the stories.

Unfortunately, too many people are trying to make a living to stay alive or watch television and sports. They do not realize what is going on behind the scenes around the world. Until they forget about entertainment that they are all bombarded with, and begin to start thinking seriously about why they are here for, and until people realize they are looking at a movie with great actors. Until humans wake up and begin to take back the Sovereignty of their own minds.

Every human on Earth must be awakened and make the necessary changes within themselves to be able to transition and be transformed by the Light.

CHAPTER 46
Time To Reclaim Your Own Sovereignty

I was walking in the middle of the woods, a door opened and a tall man, very well-mannered with a warm but sweet voice appeared in front of me and told me:

"I am here to ask you to deliver that message to your people. To be the masters of their own Universe.

As workers of Light that they are, they have to go ahead of the crowd. They occupy a position of immense power. However, that does not mean they are above you or below anyone else. Tell them that they are part of the great being called by God, or the Ones and they can manifest the wonderful New World for all of them, enjoy, and finally reap the rewards of their inner work.

The battle is already won, even though they keep hearing news of rules, regulations and blockages due to the new strains of disease, and the media keeps broadcasting fear. Do not listen, it is just tales.

Now is the time to invent their own story. It is time to move forward and live in the Fifth Dimension of love, peace, and harmony.

It is time to manifest all their desires in life. They may feel trapped by their own rules and regulations but be loved. But since these are not of the light they will see many changes and restructuring of those Governments as they all moved to the Light.

Darkness becomes light and emerges from the shadows to be healed. Darkness will not and can't survive the 5th Dimension, which is already here, not in the distant future.

Your people have the power to change the reality and in doing so, change the reality of those around them. They must understand that they can change and help those around them. Illuminating it all with their own Light. Tell them to just be. They are beacons of Light and are gathering others to follow.

Souls group is uniting right now to change the reality on Earth and at the same time change the world. Your people must trust and believe in their sovereignty and confront those who seek to take power and dominate them. Surround those who fight them in Love, for that is that is the greatest power on Earth. To love like Angels.

As their worlds are falling apart, many people on Earth are feeling anger and confusion. Darkness is coming to the surface to be healed, and some people suffer their own anger.

Therefore, let them see the light, for they do not know what they are doing. People must send them love. Not fear because as they ascend others will follow, and they will attract new friends of the same dimension. Much of the disease and evil caused by the so-called virus is caused by the same belief in the harm it can cause.

As beings that they are, they must believe in their own power to heal themselves and those around them. The wicked that has been spreading fear all over the world will not enter the 5th Dimension. Fear not, beloved, for you are not evil.

As the ray of Light that bathes the Earth begins suddenly to awaken, so to speak. And they will be able to help and guide them. Your people have been in the shadows for too long, and it's time for them to step in the front.

Now is the time to claim their sovereignty. They are the owners of the Universe. They are the future.

They must have faith in their sovereignty. Much love and Light to you all."

Said the man. And I walked out the door back in the wood with the message I have to deliver now.

CHAPTER 47
Events that Lead to Real Disclosure

It happened during the week that preceded the Olympic games in Paris, France.

In the lobby of my Hotel Boulevard Haussmann in Paris, I was waiting for my friend when I saw a young Asian couple. The man was hiding his eyes behind Dark glasses looking at me intensively while walking. The woman was elegant and thin, and she was very nice-looking. The grey color of their skin and their unusual height attracted my attention. They walked towards the elevator and just before entering it the woman turned her head looking in my direction and shapeshifted into the most hideous evil face I ever saw in my life.

I knew Aliens have been among us for thousands of years, living peacefully beneath the Earth, in the skies and among humans. I also knew there are good and bad Aliens like there are good and bad spirits.

That very evening, as I left my body I saw a very disruptive scene. I saw that there is a plan for an Alien invasion that will happen during the war in Ukraine. It will happen with both sides of the military. Black and white hats have prepared some operations that will shock the world.

These events must happen and will be stopped in the end. It will reveal the true technology hidden by the governments that control the population, and it will expose the globalist killing machine of the CIA, Pentagon operators, and the dark Generals. These will lead to the events of military occupation.

In the end, the fake Alien invasion of the project will bring down the CIA, the world's deep states black ops, and the dark operations. All this will lead to military tribunals on a world scale. For the mass murder of the world population through the creation of the virus, the earth vaccines, and the project operation fear panic death false flag event.

I saw Washington DC underwater.

The shapeshifter woman never came out of the elevator, The man stood up from his seat and finally left.

CHAPTER 48
Three Missiles Launched

I remember that evening clearly. We were expecting heavy rain and due to the bad weather, a tropical storm hit us. I was finishing dinner with Agnes when the phone rang. I heard CHADD saying, "There are 3 missiles launched" and he hung up. I tried to call him back. I wanted to understand what that was for, but he did not answer. I knew CHADD well enough to know that he was trying to tell me something important was about to happen.

Suddenly I begin to feel the terrible pressure on my upper stomach. It builds up very quickly to the point that I thought I would pass out by the pain. That is when I saw Agnes entering a trance and she began to speak.

"VIE it is not a normal attack. Jack, from the Galactic Federation, had to stop the missiles and he had no choice, he says, he is sorry, but he had to use you. It will not last long, only eighteen more minutes."

The pain was so intense at that point, that I called CHADD again. Before it even rang CHADD was on the phone. I asked him rapidly to help me with the severe pain I was having. He just said, "I will pray for you" and hung up. Effectively the pain went rapidly away.

Then Agnes still in a trance continued "Jack used you to send back the missiles from where it came using you. He needed your energy to accomplish that task.

Jack could not communicate with you; he went to a board meeting in D.C. But you will speak to a man from the Library of Congress. He will tell you that Jack is known there. He went to DC to kill a part of the brain in some people inside that function there but not for the good of the people. Apparently!"

The following day CHADD called again and said "In a vision, I heard that the Iranian Minister has been killed."

Fifteen days later Mike called me to say VIE we have to go as soon as possible to the Abbey. We have to meet a Monk and a Priest. They will be at the noon mass. I feel something is about to happen.

After a few minutes, we entered the Monastery Church one Monk welcomed us into the Monastery. Mike looked at me and said: "Let me handle it, I have to speak to this Monk." He went to the Monk, and I saw them speaking but could not hear what they said. Mike came back to sit next to me and said "He will speak to the Priest. After mass the Priest will ask you to approach him, and he will anoint you."

The mass finished and the Priest anointed me. Mike and I needed to eat before heading back home. It's a two-hour drive. We found a Greek restaurant and stopped to eat. Mike ordered first and went to the table then I joined him. My attention was attracted by a man with medium size dark hair brown pants and shirt and a dark brown round flat hat, like a beret He was passing back and forth by our table, and I felt uneasy. He walked towards the bathroom at the back of the room but turned and came back to pass our table for the first time. Then they went to order but did not. I saw the waitress beginning to sweat abundantly, though we were under air conditioning. Her eyes were also weird. She looked exhausted, hot, and scared. I did not know at that point she was under psychic attack.

Mike and I, our lunch finished we drove back home. During the two-hour drive, nothing unusual happened.

I dropped Mike at his house and went directly home. That is when it hit me suddenly. I began to sweat, felt nauseous and my head started to span. I immediately understood it was a severe attack, and I had been poisoned. As it was not the first time I rapidly took two pills of activated charcoal. My head was spinning so fast I was not able to lie down, And it took about two to two and a half hours for the charcoals to take complete effect.

It's only one week later that I have an answer of who and why this happened to me. I saw this woman I met accidentally I thought, Agnes. I saw how she planned everything after she got to know me a little better. Well! that was what she thought when she tried to manipulate me. Her goal was, and it was stupidly thought that she could do it.

I saw her goal was to replace me by making me co-dependent and live my path and destiny. She thought that she could make me dependent on her and she would enjoy my life. Who would even think it is possible except her? She did not realize I was there to see her being possessed and becoming the tool of the dark. And as the nefarious energies must express first their plan, she without knowing said it out loud.

But this did not stop there, seeing that I was strong enough to relive the attack, she attacked my knees to the point I could not walk.

I am a very compassionate, patient, and loving person but I had to ban her definitively from my life. It was clear that she was refusing to turn to God.

CHAPTER 49
The "Last Supper" A Parody of Drag Queens

Entering a Gothic cathedral in the Middle Ages, I was overtaken by the towering walls lined with colonnades on either side, pointed arches and ribbed groined vaults adorning the high ceilings, and an array of stained-glass windows illuminating the space above and around me.

The entrance I took was by the left back side. I had to push open a heavy wood door magnificently carved. The three steps of pure white marble stone were worn out in the middle by so many parishioners' feet that used it.

I saw a Bishop; he was giving an oath. A warning to the Parishioners, and to the world.

"This is a warning. Once upon a time, you were very close to Jesus Christ, the Lord of Lords and the King of the Kings. Today you are denying your Jesus.

Come back to the Lord otherwise, they will be another empire that is a dragon. Rest assured it will come upon you, before you, and the entire Globe, and no one will save you. Repent before it is too late. Come back to the Lord of all. Jesus Christ of Nazareth."

The Bishop showed me the vision of an offensive ceremony for the Paris Olympics involving a parody of the Last Supper, with transsexuals, drag queens, exposed testicles and a fat blue-painted man intended to represent Dionysus, the Greek god of wine. The fat blue-painted transsexual replacing Jesus and the disciples at the Last Supper Scene replacing Jesus and the Apostles, and a scene depicting Marie-Antoinette.

There is an immense experience of confusion on the Earth now, as so many lower vibrations came to the surface to be released. Old wounding energies come to the surface to release anger, frustration, and limitations boundaries. They are all coming to the surface within your beings and within all beings to be released.

And it is causing everyone on Earth to experience a lower vibration.

I left my body to travel to a Scientific convention. The way I approached to attend their meeting was quite interesting. I passed, in the lobby in front of the conference place, a group of seven to eight men. One heard me speaking the same foreign language and introduced itself. Like if he was looking for someone who spoke and understood what they were saying. "Hey! great I found someone who speaks the same language. My name is Matteo." They were seated in a circle. I sat next to the man that found me. He was of a German type, tall light blond, and wearing glasses. On my right side was a man with very dark hair. The tall man who asked me to join them was having a scientific magazine. I took a rapid glimpse at the open page. Then I told him: Now This is exactly what I am interested in. I work the energy but in a different way than others. Matteo was a scientist working on the energy of the brain. While I was having a conversation with Matteo the man with dark hair began to put his head on my lap and hug me. Like a child will do. A very sweet and friendly energy. Then a noise brought me back into my body.

This was the day that followed another event experience. In my dream, I was experiencing unclear experiences. I could not find clarity in the decision. Except that it did not feel right. Then in the middle of the night, I received the answer, a clear picture on how to handle it and align myself back to balance and harmony. I had to draw a specific design, saying specific words in phrases addressing the obstruction to my problem, then cut it in the middle and burn it. And I had to share it with the friend I was meeting for lunch.

But this did not stop there. I met my friend the day after for lunch. She told me that in her meditation she received a weird message. She was asked to do something on a piece of paper, burn it, and mail the ashes to that person in an envelope. My dream was the answer to both. She spoke.

CHAPTER 50

Not A Global Collapse, A Perverse Industry, and A Message Sent By Eight Doctors Killed In A Crash

In my dream, the vibration came in strong and was not uncomfortable but a feeling of infinite distance and space, as if I was looking through a window.

I began to see that the Cabal created a conspiracy story to unbalance you and destabilize the world. They have been engineered to replace the entire fiat currency system globally. Now it is taking place, but they have been working on this for a thousand years. Working until they figured out how to get it done physically and everything since the year 1972.

And someone secretly recorded a speech given when they laid out the whole agenda. Since 1072 the cabal has been working to get the pieces in place to be able to flip the switch and to make it happen. And this is why it is happening now.

Everything is ramped up. Everything around is going crazy and all at one time.

They are trying to distract everybody while they pull off this magic trick.

And a wise Bishop is warning the government that the only hope is for those who wake up and open their eyes. Satan has blinded them.

Moving forward in my dream I was at the airport. Standing next to me were a group of Eight men. Not far from them, I recognized a man who was a former French Intelligence officer, divorced from a good friend. A very well-mannered person though. When he recognized me he came towards me to shake my hand and say:

"Bonjour, vous allez bien?", and quickly in a low voice said pay attention to this man not far from you on your left side and to what they are saying. Then he said, "Aurevoir VIE, a bientot! mes amities a votre famille. J'ai un avion a prendre" and left me."

As soon as he left, I turned my attention to the group. A Doctor was denouncing the side effects of the COVID-19 vaccines being used to scare people about other conditions. Speaking of "perverse industry." According to the doctor, the expensive PCR tests launched on the market to detect the monkey Pox virus are not reliable. He argues that they are now making people afraid of diseases that are side effects of the coronavirus vaccinations rash like blisters accompanied by severe pain. Also typical for herpes zoster, or shingles. Shingles is a skin disease in which the affected person develops blisters on the skin that resemble Chicken Pox. Shingles are also a known side effect of the coronavirus vaccine. And said there is also a reappearance of a large number of cancers in our patients. Monkey Pox is a cover-up!

I woke up the following day and was eating my breakfast when the phone rang. It was CHADD asking me if I heard the morning news. I said no but I had a weird dream. Of course, I haven't yet, and he said, "Well! let me read to you. Eight doctors among 62 killed in a horrifying plane crash. The plane smashed into the background of a home inside a gated community and transformed into a fiery wreck, All sixty people aboard were killed. Among them, the eight doctors and two from Uopeccan Cancer Hospital in Cascavel were among the passengers who died."

Then it suddenly struck me, and I told CHADD: I remember when I was sitting in a very luxurious tropical jungle with people on an island and I was offered some Kava Kava in an official ceremony and what Kafoa the shaman showed me in a vision. The clear and vivid vision of Dr. Ceron was found dead. His research facility was raided by the US government to seize a breakthrough cancer treatment called GcMAF.

Before being found dead, shot in the head Dr. Ceron was working telepathically with Kafoa on a little-known molecule that occurs naturally in the human body. It has also been shown to reverse signs of autism in the vast majority of patients receiving the treatment.

I remember very well asking Kafoa, Would the cancer industry go as far as to murder doctors to protect its profits? and Kafoa answered, "Yes it would. An oncologist was recently sentenced to nearly sixty years in prison for falsely diagnosing patients 'cancers so that he could sell them chemotherapy treatments they didn't need!"

So that continues, it's terrible said CHADD.

CHAPTER 51
A Battle Report of Two Thousands Reptilians Exterminated

In August the victory given against the Reptilians was effective and decisive.

I was awakened in the middle of my sleep on August 27th, and I have revealed very important information I needed to recall and so, to write.

This is what I was given to read from the United Galactic Federation of Planets.

"If you have seen yourself in recurring battles and the feeling of waking up for no reason exhausted and even sore, it is because you are one of so many warriors taking the battles. There are two thousand outside of my group who accompany us to the battles.

The Brothers of Light look in all countries for the warriors of Light humans who are asleep and annex them to the battles.

The battle has been fought in two ways creating a mantle of Light over each country that upon contact with every dark being is liquidated.

The mantle started in Venezuela, from there spread to Canada, Argentina and Brazil. Two thousand million Reptilians have already been liquidated. From there passed to Europe, Yugoslavia, Italy, and now France. The mantle of Light will cover all of Europe. It's a battle tactic given by the United Galactic Federation of Planets.

Taking advantage of the mantle of Light in Italy my warriors entered the Vatican and found it creepy, mined of Reptilians, many Hybrids. It was given battle there and we found a material that gave us information about the location of the heads of these dark races in the depths of the planet. They have all been exterminated.

Concerning Nuclear Research and CERN. CERN will resume its research of a lead particle ion very soon. A ritual has been observed in front of the Hindu Deity Lord Shiva, the Hindu God of storms and destruction who is fear-inducing!

CHAPTER 52
Planetary Liberation Report

The adventure never stops. Knowledge is a blessing, not a curse. You must learn to be sensitive to the voice within. Allow images, messages, or another form of guidance to surface and help you navigate better. In the process involving me, the source energy, and you.

I just received this new and important message from Archangel Michael to be shared with you. "We want to see this planet free! We as a special force are in charge of the protection of these enemy forces from the planet for its liberation.

The planet is in rather an unstable situation, my loved ones. The electronic field is rather distorted. We know that we are entering into a spiral where there is a lot of turbulence. The elements are being activated, wind, water and earth are all being activated. This whole transformation is an integrated process. The teams are providing a helping hand.

Powerful energies are arriving on the planet! As you know, portals and portals are open, which were opened to prevent them from closing! The planet is moving forward in an ascension spiral, and we are going higher and higher in the system. The entire solar system is moving forward, and the planet as a whole, along with the whole system. We help you through the whole process at every level. We pay special attention to planet

Earth in this special project designed by Mother Adonai for humanity given the great intervention suffered by the opposing and enemy forces against Father Adonai which managed to enslave humanity for so long.

All the interstellar Command has given all the effort and help, support in this system, in this galaxy to make this project of Mather Father move towards its happy boarding.

There are a few of them left, but they are reluctant, they know they have to go because they can no longer tolerate this frequency they have installed on the planet.

Their clones are controlled by artificial intelligence that they control. many of these you see are all artificial intelligence controlled from their control centers.

They have no feelings; they have no love. They have no conscience and no compassion.

Many think that people are gone and gone, but we have saved those who could be saved and brought them on ships, especially the twelve ships that are responsible for the whole process of preparing souls and beings for evolutionary processes.

Time is rushing everything is moving forward, everything is accelerating. They want to destroy everything before they leave; these are instructions. Their planetary representatives, perhaps some in physical bodies, are also exposed to these systems, all they have done and installed in their bodies to obey the Great Master.

Nothing left of them on this planet! We will not be rested, happy, or content until we see the last remnants of this darkness that has kept you enslaved for so long!

You will be free, completely free.

The new Earth waits for you, a liberated Earth, freed from this slavery and this negativity, We are fighting against them in body and soul in every being, in every dimension, in every manifestation of the flesh on every level because they seek to infiltrate where we least think.

We are almost at the end of the process of singing the ultimate victory of the liberation of the planet, but remember first of all, free yourselves, each of you, internally, from all the old programming that has been forced upon you by the old system of control, and expand your hearts of light, love, and peace towards.

Peace must rule the planet, in your hearts, and will fight for the peace of the planet.

Do not let those provokers think that they will be able to start a war on the planet, because we will not allow it to happen to them at all.

Take care of your emotional and mental bodies. The blue team of Archangel Michael is paying attention to every call, do not allow yourself to become victims of parasites.

Cleanse and liberate yourself daily because of these energies, these beings are in despair and are attacking.

Humanity has already understood, opened its awareness, understanding, and awakened many things, but they are still unaware of how powerful these negative forces are and what they can extract you from your energy field.

That's why we tell you to protect yourselves every day and stay safe. You will be rid of all this barbarism and all this negativity very soon.

I am Archangel Michael; I bless you all and we are at your service. We want this planet to be free, free, free soon.

CHAPTER 53

The Encounter with a Guardian's Spirit

The night had fallen over the island and the sky were filled with countless stars twinkling like diamonds. A group of people has set up camp on the Pines Island beach around a fire in front of the ocean. Their faces were illuminated by the dancing flames. The water splashing on the sand whispers ancient secrets.

The elders in the group were telling stories of the guardians. Their tales speak of guidance and protection. Suddenly the wind started blowing, then ceased as suddenly as it blew. The flames of the fire began to flicker.

Out of the shadows, a voice emerges. It was a being made of Light; its body surrounded by a faint glowing aura.

"Who are you?" asked one of the elders. They could hear a calm powerful voice speaking. "I am a spirit from the guardians sent to watch over you. We have been here since the beginning of time, and we are still watching.

Everyone sat in silence, overwhelmed by what they had just experienced. They knew their lives would never be the same again after. For they had encountered a guardian's spirit, and it had revived a promise of protection and guidance that would follow them all their days.

I realized I was part of the group of people and had also encountered the guardian's spirit and received the promise of protection before receiving important information. CHADD though not physically was present, and we could exchange telepathically.

"The first contact process has begun! 5Dimension has changed forever. There is Light inside all. We will help people reach the Light. It is a human time. The divine process has begun. It is a turning point in history and transformation of events called a timeline.

Humanity is in a timeline where something is going to happen; that is in this age of the Universe, major events are taking place which can be called a historical turning point. Earth is moving from 3D to 5D, and Souls currently incarnated on Earth are now also moving their ascension.

Only one-third of humanity is able to achieve and complete the ascend necessary for this transition. The other half is not. Though it is the most important time in the entire history of the Planet or even the Universe. But above all the greatest moment on Earth is the awakening of mankind.

The ancient prophecies of Armageddon do not come true! (It is a prophecy that describes a final battle between forces of good and evil. Mentioned in the New Testament, in Revelation to John, or the Apocalypse of St. John (16:16), The name Armageddon is likely derived from Hebrew and means "Hill of Megiddo". It is symbolic of the progression of the world toward the "Great day of God", the Almighty, in which God pours out his just and holy wrath against unrepentant sinners led by Satan.

Heaven, there are still major obstacles that affect the destiny of mankind, but right now is the defining moment for mankind on Planet Earth with two New Timelines that will determine the future. One will bring a part of humanity to the new Earth in 5D, the other will bring the rest into exile to another Planet in 3D.

At some point, a New Cycle and a New Earth will emerge, where there will be no authority or superiority to influence our free will decisions. Everyone will be his own judge. No one will interfere in others' individual decisions.

The Light has won, and everyone creates their reality. Humanity's fate has finally been decided. The wheat has been separated. Only Five-dimensional beings will go to the Five-dimension New Earth. This process is to be completed, clarified, and resolved within 5 months from now. By the end of this year.

The Light is getting more intense making it impossible for sleepers to fully sleep. It is certain that many, even if awakened by high intensity of Light, will choose another dark Planet to continue their deep soul slumber."

CHAPTER 54

Two Races of Greys' Demons

Seven months now since we, CHADD and VIE had to only communicate by phone for our protection, and luckily we have telekinesis.

I lay down and turned myself on my left side. At first, it looked like a bright circle, but it soon began to have more depth. A brightly shining light appeared. I blinked twice and refocused.

You see said CHADD, they do not know that long, long ago, far beyond the edges of recorded time the ancient once lived in a state of balance, aware that their thoughts, intentions, and actions were ripples in the fabric of existence. It was affecting not only their world but the stars and systems beyond.

But we are not alone on Earth. Many races walked alongside them. These races had come from various corners of the Universe seeking a fertile world, for Earth was a unique gem among the many in the cosmos. A library of life and knowledge. However, the tranquility and flourishing of this epoch were not to last and the skies darkened.

The greys are the Illuminati and the controllers. They are both demons and they both kill humans to survive. Their missions are to fool and distract mankind from moving forward and evolving into higher vibrations.

One grey needs the blood of human beings and the other takes a sort of bath in the liquified bodies. So, they made a deal on Earth and passed a law that allowed them to liquefy dead bodies. They harvest the blood of children and liquefy the adult bodies. They kidnap children and adults for that purpose.

The Earth's military is split in two. The one that honors and serves their country and the others. The good part of the military is based on some troops in various galaxies and has a hundred and fifty spaceships. They battle the greys and kill them to defend humanity against these demons that can only survive through the liquified bodies and the blood of children.

Extraterrestrials on Earth Aid Service. There are a lot of people here in aid service on Earth. They left their own universe learning to help on this planet where they are also learning but decided to come to help give their support to humanity and maybe a lot of people can choose to, they return as soon as their purpose has been fulfilled. And those who have learned anything go to the world of excuses to continue learning.

Here is how some of these people who came to service on Earth explain various subjects.

The Two Crystalline Tablets of Nano Material and Moses. "Accorded to the Bible, the first set of tablets were inscribed by the finger of God, (Exodus 31:18) and were smashed by Moses when he was enraged by the sight of the Children of Israel worshiping a golden calf (Exodus 32:19) and the second were later chiseled out by Moses and rewritten by God (Exodus 34:1)."

Moses went up on the Mont Sinai. He had an encounter with an extraterrestrial, and he was given the knowledge. The knowledge was inscribed in what you may call tablets, but it was not in stone.

The tablets were made of a kind of crystalline formation, a kind of crystalline nanomaterial with information that was downloadable information with the touching of your hand. Like a touchable screen. There was some information in it, but only in the most general sense of categories of this. You will touch here, and it will get that knowledge, and you will touch here, and it will get you this other knowledge, etc…

The Nuclear Research. The European Organization for Nuclear Research and the Cern. A large Hadron Collider (LHC) 27-kilometer ring of superconducting magnets accelerates particles to near light speed that collide together. The collision produces massive particles. The World's largest and highest-energy particle collider and most powerful particle accelerator.

The CERN has announced that it will resume its research of lead particle ions very soon. During these activities, it is suggested portals are opened and some strange site things are occurring. A ritual is taking place in front of the "Hindu Deity Lord Shiva" the God of storms and destruction who is fear-inducing.

Aborted fetus and the Pineal Gland: The spirit and the soul cannot fully connect to the body for forty-nine days. That is the time the pineal gland forms. Then the idea of full consciousness comes through the body.

There are Gang members and migrants that invade a small town, abduct pets, and eat them. A woman has been seen by the police and has been arrested covered in blood was eating a cat.

But all the negative forces that kept humanity in such a capacity and wanted to disrupt the process will receive their "Reward". Because they will be brought before the Cosmic Court according to the universal laws, and this process is about to be closed and terminated.

But they still want to drag it away reinvent themselves, and try to prevent the humanity of Adonai, in the genetic of Adam Kadmon in this dense body, which is not so dense. This is a reminder and call for people, to work internally until the last moment. To free themselves, raise their energy vibration, and connect with the Christ inside them.

Energy is all given to help their plan. Everything helps them. The sun's energy, the portals, and all the star systems have sent their representation to help. The squad from Underground City all. Everything is organized because this is the plan of Adonai. They should keep working because every step you take in the frequency is for their profit. People should not gamble and they will gain this by healing themselves, by the energy that is sent to them.

CHAPTER 55
The 7 Dimension Crystal Line Light Body and Brain, and the Precursors

As I watch it feels like I am looking at the universe. There is nothing around me, I feel like I am floating again. Now I get it, it looks like the whole cosmos. Like being full of planets and stars.

We are currently preparing for the next phase of human evolution, which will be the sixth, root race of Humankind. We are gradually transforming from carbon-based to crystal-based. The metamorphosis will occur at the cellular level.

Many Lightworkers are now preparing for their seventh-dimensional light bodies. This happens because the body contains a higher wage of light, which contains love, knowledge, and wisdom.

This is the ascension journey. In the new high-frequency bodies and brain, the atoms are arranged according to sacred geometry, activating the crystal structure.

Sometimes people think crystal line means hard like crystal. However, it indicates that the new crystalline people will get will have qualities of crystal. Our crystalline bodies will be healthier and stronger with much greater physical capacity than our current ones.

Currently, we have a right and left-brain hemisphere. As we evolve, this will no longer be the case.

The left cerebral half will be replaced by a crystalline brain that will be like an advanced personal computer, with huge memory storage and the ability to perform complex calculations, great creativity and incredible abilities. Everyone will be able to see through dimensions, allowing everyone to connect with the elemental and angelic realms, as well as the great masters and star beings from across the universe.

The right brain half becomes the heart. New children are already being born with twelve strands of DNA fully connected. As they are activated and their crystalline brain develops, we will be amazed by their incredible gifts and power.

Many adults in the Fifth begin to develop their higher-dimensional light bodies and brains in preparation for the next phase.

To prepare for this absorb more light, eat lighter foods, drink clean water, connect with nature, and do proper exercises. Watch your thoughts, words, and actions, and make sure they are positive. Meditate and do ascension exercises. Relax and breathe well. All these things affect you on a cellular level and affect the quality of light you emit.

We are all so blessed to be here during this time of metamorphosis on Earth as we enter the new and exciting energies of the golden future.

The perfect human of the golden future. In preparation for the golden future on Earth, we begin to remember and harness the gifts and powers we have developed in Atlantis. In the past, everyone had gifts and powers that we now find extraordinary, but gifts such as clairvoyance, healing telepathy, but also self-healing, were considered very normal. The forces of teleportation mind control, telekinesis, levitation, and manifestation were developed through deep relaxation and mind control. It also meant understanding the frequencies of light and sound.

The Precursors walk among you that look like you, but they have a different frequency than you. they go about the planet Earth from time to time walking through the cities and countryside and when you might sometimes pass by them, they observe to see if you can tell that they are not from your world. That is used as a measurement of your sensitivity and your readiness to interact with beings from other civilizations. That is the job of the precursors. So that will increase and especially it will increase in the fulcrum of two thousand and twenty-seven.

CHAPTER 56

War is the Destroyer of Oneness and the Thought is the Fastest Laser Known

On that third Saturday of the month, I was meeting my new friend Ximena for lunch. The minute we entered the restaurant I felt his energy. The energy of the man. I turned my head to the left and there he was looking at us coming inside. His elbow on the table in front of him and his head resting on his arm, his face turned toward us. He looked at me intensively. He was of middle size in his mid-thirties with a T-shirt and a Blue Jean.

"Are you religious?" he said.

"Do I know you?" I said.

"No," he replied.

"Sorry, yes, yes but from another lifetime.

"Ok", I said. And then he said: "Because religion has conveniently been a wonderful mask for war on the planet. But war is the great destroyer of Oneness. If you link the soul and war, then the soul will never fully grow. The soul is then trapped when it is under the influence of war."

Suddenly, I hear loud and clear CHADD saying "Intertwined". It intertwines VIE if you allow war to be associated with spirit and soul. Such as in holy wars. You empower war and give war an even more almighty power on Earth. War is convenient for those who want to keep humans in their place because war creates fear, destruction, and most importantly separation. Wisdom and spiritual wisdom, in particular, help to create and enhance emotional maturity. People have been disconnected from their spiritual wisdom, told what to think and what to believe.

Then the man in the restaurant continued: People have been taught to consider crazy or conspiratorial anything outside the mainstream narrative that has been wired into their system.

The prophets have warned that the Earth will experience great turmoil, wickedness, war, and suffering. The prophet Daniel (12:1) said that the time before the second coming world would be a time of trouble such as the Earth has never known.

Before Christ returns five things will happen.

1. Restorations of the State of Israel.
2. The rise of Russia.
3. The word of God states that the Roman Empire (once a European Kingdom) will be reborn one day. Daniel 7:7.
4. The rise of worldwide Lawlessness. Before the return of the Christ, there will also be an intensified increase of Lawlessness that has not been seen the days of Sodom and Gomorrah. We will see many of those call themselves Christians and will be lawless and defiled. There all come in the last days scoffers, waking after their own lusts. The rise of lawlessness will separate the Godly from the wicked.
5. We are going to see the greatest revival since Pentecost. Acts 3:19-21, "Repent Ye therefore, and be converted, that your sins may be wiped out, when the times of refreshing shall come from the presence of the Lord; And He shall send

Jesus-Christ, which before was preached into you. Whom the beacon must receive until the times of restitution of all things, which God has spoken by the mouth of all his holy prophets since the world began."

The Lord's Victorious return is the fulfillment of the Bible prophecy, The Eastern gate, in the old city of Jerusalem, has been seated for centuries, According to prophecy, it will be reopened one day as Jesus-Christ the King of Glory, returns. And nothing can hinder that glorious day! The prophecy has foretold it, and the signs are everywhere. Jesus-Christ is coming soon.

Then CHADD voice came again and said: Thought is much faster than sound and much faster than Light and thought. Thought is the fastest laser Known. That is why, we must advise the people to watch out their thoughts. They do not want to manifest something negative.

You see, I continued, the controllers and self-elected stupidly try to separate us as we the God Duo brings you oneness. Christ consciousness, and knowledge of events including humanity evolution.

Today we live in a time where no one wants the truth heard, and people reject the truth. They prefer to stay comfortable ignoring it. The truth hurts, the truth upsets, it perturbs, and everything is made in the actual society to hide the truth. All is made to hide the truth and keep people unaware of what is happening in the meantime.

CHADD may still be forcibly leaving by court order with Katherine and Paul's Hybrids and forced to ingest pharmaceutical drugs, but we still communicate another way. No body can separate the God Duo.

Our time of reunion is coming soon. It is getting closer. The father said. three are already gone and three more hybrids soon to be.

CHAPTER 57

Unaware That I Am Participating To An Underground Experience

As I lay down to sleep, the feeling surged into my head and swept over my entire body. It was a steady vibration unvarying in frequency. I stay calm with it. I could see the room around me, but I could hear a little above the roaring sound caused by the vibrations. At that point, I wondered what would happen next.

The winter was coming, and the chill of winter air was apparent. I wanted a nice warm meal. A few minutes after I was seated at the table I saw in a corner Agnes seated having a drink. That is where my first painful and weird event happened. It really took me by surprise, and I had no idea, no clue what was happening.

My environment and personal experiences had led me to expect some kind of answer. But no, I was facing something where answers were not quickly available. I had determined that there was no physiological cause. The answer takes the form of rationalization, if it can be called that; or more commonly, the form of a search I made of past memories and experiences.

That happened as I was waiting for my meal at the table with Agnes seated in front of me. A group of six to seven people entered the room. I immediately caught on the middle-aged man, medium height, tan complexion with dark hair and dark glasses coming with the group. It was obvious that he was trying not to be seen by me and was walking looking at the floor. Then I suddenly felt his heavy energy. I immediately stood up and left the room telling my friend, while already heading out, to follow me. I had to leave, and she should do the same, I said to her. I barely had the time to exit and get in my car when I was seized with a severe, iron-hard cramp that extended across my diaphragm area just under my rib cage. It was like a solid band of unyielding aches. At first, I thought that it was some food poisoning. I still could breathe normally in spite of the unbearable pain. I had no other symptoms, just hard tense, locked-in-place rigidity of a band of muscles in my upper abdomen.

This was my first out-of-ordinary physical event of the sort that took place. And I heard Agnes saying to me "It will stop in 10 minutes now" I did not really pay attention to what she said thinking she was trying to reassure me.

One week later, the second major event happened. When my body was struck my entire body shook violently. These happened in the same peculiar conditions and at different conditions.

An invisible ray seemed to have come from the sky to strike my body, and Agnes was with me again when her voice said this second time it happened "It will last twenty minutes more. And be aware that it will happen again in the future two or three times, after today." The twenty minutes passed, the sensation and the pain faded away and I got up off my chair feeling perfectly normal.

That is when I remembered the man that I was introduced to by Agnes at a convention I attended, invited by her. And I happened to meet this man again in a group meeting. Agnes asked me to go with her. When I met the man the second time was also present a woman, named Graziella. I remember that she read my energy without my consent and pretended to know me.

Three weeks later Graziella had researched and found my phone number. She called me and asked me to join their next Saturday group meeting saying, "Your energy would make a big difference for us to grow and achieve our goal quicker" Of course my intuition told me not to and I did not go. After all, I did not know these people.

It was a month later that I discovered that some experiments were done by a group of people living on an underground base.

To my astonishment, I had participated without my consent or knowledge in an experience initiated by what became apparently an underground group that started more than one hundred years ago. When present-day science began to organize man's concepts and rid them of unreasoning, or unsupported "Knowledge".

Every person, object, animal, plant, and form as well as each sensation, emotion, thought, and state of being has a unique frequency. My vibration, as yours, communicates with who you are and helps you shape our reality. Your vibration is powerful. It is the key to transformation. Our vibration, identity, and reality are continually adapting to keep pace as we are transforming.

These two events lead me to guide you to learn to protect yourself with energy shielding protection.

Energy shielding Protection will give you freedom. You can do it anywhere and be with anyone you choose with no toxic consequences. Designing protection lets you exist in your clear energy and allows the world to be your protecting shell. It is said that by making a shield, you also signal to the universe that you believe in its trusted guidance. There are different ways to do it.

One is to visualize you in the spiritual color fuchsia. The second one is to make yourself invisible. The third one is the energy shielding protection technique.

Imagine yourself in a sacred geometry shape. Then tap into the energy of Gold. If it does not fit you play with colors. White, or try purple, violet, or green. Visualize it. You may hear the color or feel it. Or smell it.

Once you have connected with the right color, imagine a stream coming down from a haven that fills up your sacred geometry shape. For some, the color will simply fill your body, and it is fine. Play with the colors as some of you may use multiple colors.

You will then feel energized, and calm, maybe feel some tingling. Set your intention for the day, visualize yourself in sacred geometry, bask in your color and your shield is complete.

Everything is a lesson, even to remind yourself to protect yourself. It took me some time to find out who Agnes was and her intention. The poison is the first attack at the restaurant and the man in dark glasses, the second after visiting the monastery, and the third in the underground all orchestrated by Agnes. But where she finally burns herself was when she dropped her own protection, when she thought I would by now never suspect her. That day I had an important meeting. I visited a house for sale. Suddenly I became totally drained and as time passed, I could not walk anymore. The minute I realized what was happening, I could put it all together. That made me remember that the very first time she invited me to join her for lunch I was poisoned.

I texted Agnes, "Do not try to communicate with me anymore. Go and get an exorcism." She tried after a week to reconnect with me. She texted me, "Maybe it will not work for me." Of course, I deleted it immediately. Another week later, she called me and left a message. I deleted it without listening to it.

CHAPTER 58
Truth is Detergent to the New World Order

The dream becomes more and more realistic. What was happening was real. The next-door house was invaded, I was in my house upstairs looking by the window and seeing everything, but I realized that I could be seen.

When entering the room, I thought that I involuntarily hit the Light switch. I tried to switch it off but never could. Of course, I can only enlighten!

If you know, understand that knowledge is control and control is freedom. Truth is detergent to NWO.

There are a lot of people here in aid service. They left their own world; they left their own universal learning to help on this planet where they are also learning. But they decided to come help and give support to humanity, and maybe a lot of people can choose too that they return as soon as their proposal has been fulfilled. And those who have learned anything go to the world of excuses to continue learning.

All those negative forces that kept you in such a capacity and wanted to disrupt the process will receive their reward because they will be brought before the cosmic court according to the universal laws. The process is now about to be closed and terminated. But still, they want to drag it away and reinvent themselves. To present the humanity of Father-Mother Adonai, in the genetic of Adam Kadmon in this dense body, which is not so dense. This is a reminder and a call for you, to work internally until the last moment, to free yourself and raise your frequency vibration. Connect with the Christ being in your beings!

Everything is all given to help you plan. Everything helps you. The sun's energy, the portals, and all the star systems have sent their representation to help. Squad from underground city, all. Everything is organized because this is the plan of Adonai. Keep working, because every step you take in the frequency is a profit for you. Don't gamble and you gain this by healing yourself with the energies that are sent to help you.

For an aborted fetus, you must know that the spirit, the soul, cannot fully connect to the body for 49 days. That is the time the pineal gland forms, (852 Hz). Then the idea of full consciousness comes through the body, Nevertheless, the spirit, the being knows what the decision will be. It only wanted to have a brief experience of the physical reality. Nothing happens by accident. It is an orchestration. That being still exists, is perfectly viable, and still loves you. He knew and wanted to give the mother an experience in that sense chose to help the mother. All spirits, all beings are eternal.

We are currently preparing for the next phase of human evolution, which will be the sixth root race of humankind. We are gradually transforming from carbon-based to crystal-based. The metamorphosis will occur at the cellular level. Many Lightworkers are now preparing for their 7th-dimensional light bodies. This happens because the body contains a higher wage of light, which contains love, knowledge, and wisdom. This is the journey to ascension.

In the new high-frequency bodies and brains, the atoms are arranged according to sacred geometry, activating the Crystal structure. Sometimes people think crystal line means hard like crystal. However, it indicates that the new crystalline people will have the qualities of a crystal. Our crystalline bodies will be healthier and stronger with much greater physical capacity than our current ones.

Currently, we have a right and left-brain hemisphere, As we evolve, this will no longer be the case. The half-left cerebral will be replaced by a crystalline brain that will be like an advanced personal computer with huge memory storage and the ability to perform complex calculations, great creativity and incredible abilities. Everyone will be able to see through dimensions, allowing everyone to connect with the elemental and angelic realms, as well as the great masters and star beings from across the Universe. The half-right brain becomes the heart.

Today children are born with 12 stands of DNA fully connected. As they are activated and their crystalline brain develops, we will be amazed by their incredible gifts and power.

Many adults in the 5th dimension begin to develop their higher-dimensional light bodies and brains in preparation for the next phase. To prepare for this and absorb more light, eat lighter foods, drink clean water, connect with nature, and do proper exercises. Watch your thoughts, words, and actions, and make sure they are positive. Meditate and do ascension exercises. Relax and breathe well. All of these things affect the quality of light you emit. We are so blessed to be here during this time of metamorphosis on Earth as we enter the new and exciting energies of the golden future.

The perfect human of the golden future. In preparation for the golden future on Earth, we begin to remember and harness the gifts and powers we have developed in Atlantis. In the past, everyone had gifts and powers that we now find extraordinary, but gifts such as clairvoyance, healing, telepathy, but also self-healing, were considered normal.

The forces of teleportation, mind control telekinesis, levitation and manifestation were developed through deep relaxation and miscontrol. It also meant understanding the frequencies of Light and Sound. As we, Doctor of Sound Frequencies CHADD and Doctor of Light Frequency Vibrations VIE understand.

So don't be too shocked when you begin perceiving other beings that others may say are not there.

CHAPTER 59
The Story of Isadora and 396 Shuman HZ Releases Fear

I drove up to the restaurant where I was meant to have lunch with Isadora and her friend Sophia. I parked, stepped out of the car and walked toward the entrance of the Colombian restaurant. As I walked towards the entrance of Don Juan Alexandro restaurant thoughts and questions filled my mind. Was Sophia coming with Isadora and in the same car?

The inside of the restaurant was packed. I walked up the steps and became aware of the crowd. Looking around I was taken by surprise when I saw waving at me, Emma. What are you doing here? I said to Emma. Emma replied, "My intuition told me you would be here, and I decided to join you. I took a long meditation this morning and it led me here."

Hum! I thought she had again done some clairvoyance and picked on me. Look Emma I said, "You cannot read people's minds. You have to stop doing this immediately. Then I saw Isadora entering alone and walking towards me. I had no choice but to introduce them, Isadora had a pink top like she said. She looked at me with a big smile and hugged me.

Let's get to the table she said, Sophia is caught in traffic. She should be here shortly. We sat and Isadora began to talk.

"I joined the team of real estate just to meet you. I have asked the Universe to send me a holistic person. And here you are. I manifest my thoughts very quickly. I was so excited when I read your e-mail. I could feel the love through the text while reading it."

Then she looked at her phone, read a message she received, excused herself and walked away from the table. "I'll be right back, she said" She came back to the table not even three minutes later and said "Sophia is apologizing herself. She is parking right now." Then I saw Sophia entering the restaurant. Isadora quickly went up and walked towards the entrance and both came to the table. Sophia had a big smile on her face, though I did not know her yet, and hugged me saying "Isadora told me so much about you and the way you both met."

That's when I had vivid visions and received the truth about Emma. Why and how she managed to meet me to fulfill her own purpose. She understood the danger to her project when I met Isadora and Sophia. Well! she thought was. She did not know she could not steal from me of my destiny and path. Emma knew from CHADD and I, that the 396 Shuman HZ releases Fear, panic, guilt, and judgements... she understood our power with the knowledge. But she thought she could stop CHADD and I from guiding and working with Isadora's son, and Sophia.

CHAPTER 60

The Return of the Summarian Enlil

I finally fell asleep when I awoke at 3:30 am receiving a great deal of information on great disasters.

The Allien fallen angel. The return of the Summarian Enlil God of wind and destruction. In the biggest office building in the world serving as the Head Quarter Department of Defense, the symbol of military strength, the military in the know covers the return of the Summarian God Enlil. The alien and a fallen angel, Enlil God of the atmosphere, the wind and storm.

In November 12 a disturbing commercial was aimed, depicted by some psychopaths with pyramid makes physically abusing babies by using them as musical instruments.

Five years later on February 6th an earthquake occurred, and an action was created. October of the following year Hurricane Helene was a devastating tropical cyclone that caused widespread destruction.

In late September of the same year a devastated in western North Carolina, less than two weeks after a major hurricane posed an extremely serious threat and was another created action magnetically stirred from underground the sunshine state, with two more spinning in the Atlantic.

The first hurricane took place where the largest amount of lithium in the world is located.

(Lithium is used in rechargeable batteries for mobile phones, laptops, digital cameras, and electric vehicles. Lithium is also used in drugs that treat bipolar disorder.)

The second hurricane was an attempt to submerge and destroy the US Department of Defense headquarters.

On October 25, my intuition told me to visit the Divine Mercy Chapel and be present to participate in the 3 PM Divine Mercy Prayer, given to Sister Faustina for the end of time. Driving back home I received from an unknown woman a message on a video saying that the Cabal wanted to eliminate Florida from the Map! But the Lord intervened then the woman said:

"Hey everyone! Yesterday a little after 11:30 PM, the Lord just gave me a message and I need to come on and share it with you as soon as I can. So, I was just in prayer with my husband and the Lord began to show me a vision. In this vision, I saw which President is winning the election, and then I saw the celebrations take off all across the US. Once I saw that I heard the Lord say that He, the Lord, will give the US a short window of time to repent. Yes, a small window that the Lord is giving to us to be able to reach the lost. To be able to reach the ones that are to be saved. Listen, the Lord said that America needs to do a national day of repentance. So, I am telling you, and giving you the message, that in America every believer who calls themselves by the name of Jesus needs to have a day of repentance. Get on your knees and seek God, and you have to cry out to him for repentance for the nation. Your Prayers must be directed to Washington DC full of snakes and demons and addressed these prayers to the Trinity asking for forgiveness and begging and crying to the Father to intervene and save the lost souls. He is giving us a small window. Continue praying that He will allow His will to be done as it is in heaven. President Trump will have a second term. Stay in prayer continue praying, and fasting the Lord will intervene in Jesus' name. I love all of you. Have a blessed day. Have a blessed night"

I had just finished telling people around when the phone rang, and I heard CHADD saying what are you doing? I am just checking on you.

Then now it was Marc saying they were trying to destroy Disney, they should stop, they should leave Disney alone.

I kept saying Marc, Marc, what is going on? Then He hung up. I tried calling him back, but the phone picked up, but no one was talking.

CHAPTER 61
A Quantum Leap Evolution. Becoming Immortal

Suddenly I stopped, or I was stopped. I was in a rather dark room. Someone was holding me very still in a standing position. After a moment of waiting, a white cloud seemed to blow through a small hole in the floor. The cloud took form, and some sense told me it was my spiritual friend from behind the veil although I could not see him too well. He spoke immediately

"Humanity will be immortal and there will be no death on the Earth. It will be a paradise place. The conversion from carbon-based DNA to crystal-based DNA. It is a quantum leap in human evolution.

Humanity is becoming immortal and will soon be entering a new world. Entering soon the new heaven and the new Earth. The new Earth exists in the same place as the old Earth but at a higher level. The energy of the Earth's two mountains influences humanity and moves to the new Heaven and the new Earth.

The consciousness of mankind rises to higher levels and spirituality develops. 5D new Heaven and new Earth is not real. It is not a real physical planet, but in a higher dimension called the fifth dimension. The old land is still dominated by light.

In the new Earth, you have a crystal-based DNA body, described as a breakthrough in human evolution. On the old Earth, you had a carbon-based body.

During the transition period, the existing carbon-based materials, are gradually replaced with lighter, crystalline materials.

These light bodies are the actual physical manifestations of the new crystal grid, which is slowly being drawn into the Earth's collective Consciousness field.

They exist in physical form like your current body, but they consist of a more sophisticated energy matrix. More in tune with the resonance frequency of the true self. The multidimensional eternal essence exists beyond time and space.

Humans are not aware of their souls and spirits because they behave like dead bodies. Humans, you, have been programmed to forget the ancient secret of immortality.

Upon arriving at Shintenshinji, you gain knowledge and become an immortal being. In ancient Earth, there was death and separation of male and female energies. There is no death but only unity, ONE. One masculine and feminine energies unite."

CHAPTER 62

The Great Angelic Master Healers

I had this powerful dream. Luxury is these little supernatural things.

Daily reality is just walking into a dimensional dream because that is simply the place that we, the God Duo CHADD and I, have evolved to.

In my dream, I am living on a beautiful ranch with horses. I was guided to visit a ranch. I immediately fell in love with the place and the location. It felt very peaceful and inviting. The ranch was beautiful. The house was nice in structure and measurement, but the inside had to be renovated and remodeled. And that was even better, I thought. As I have a very specific taste and ideas on how I see it. The house had definitively to be upgraded.

Still in the dream, I heard the invitation from the horses to come and connect with them. "You have sent us an invitation because this is a time of awakening your planet."

I went and sat on the grass under the tree not far from the pond. The house was further behind the back. The horses followed me. I sat there and entered myself while they held the space and one of them protected us. Then I listened to their energy eyes closed, and I felt their breath, and I felt them, as they felt me, and together we traveled out of space.

The heart is the most powerful generator of electromagnetic energy in the human body, producing the largest rhythmic electromagnetic field of any body's organs. The electric field is about sixty times greater in amplitude than the electrical activity generated by the brain.

The magnetic field produced by the heart is five thousand times greater in strength than the field generated by the brain and can be detected a number of feet away from the body in all directions.

A horse's heart's electromagnetic field is five times greater than yours, making their sensitivity to energies around them more acute, thus picking up the energy humans are putting out, a horse's heart beats three times slower than yours. They can assist you on many levels and layers in deep healing, fine-tuning, and removing blockages and negative energies. They help regulate your nervous system just by being there.

Human emotions carry different energies that horses will feel, and they will respond to them by showing you what you are feeling. When your heart and body connect to this energy you feel a sense of well-being, a relief and the body begins to heal inviting you to slow down and experience what is happening inside you.

I saw from the corner of my eye a line of people waiting at the entrance observing and waiting for their turn.

Looking at the person under the shadow of the three lying down on a massage table with me and the horses around her. On each side of her shoulder was a horse slightly bent, eyes closed, and I was above her head my hand working on her aurific field.

CHADD was also there observing part of it. The Healing session finished CHADD gently helped us all to be grounded and back in our bodies.

This was so powerful the nefarious energies did not like it. The truth disturbs and troubles them. A few days later we had at the location a flood zone. Luckily the water did not access the paddle and went down quickly.

CHAPTER 63
Friar Louis and the Great Solar Eclipse

CHADD was laughing, loud and happy. He had a big smile. We had arrived in an unknown place. Once again I did not realize while I was driving that he had changed the music. I had entered a trance and traveled elsewhere. But I could see from where I was an obscure Monastery in the background, and I was trying to decide what to do, when a man approached us.

"I am from the Monastery, and I am here to help you," he said. We both turned to see the man standing nearby, watching.

He spoke in a strong voice, heavy with sarcasm. "Well, now are you ready to hear the secrets of the Cosmic event?"

I masked my embarrassment by asking who he was. "Brother Louis," he shouted. I am with the congregation you can see from here. I also got the impression that he was calling us by our names. Hum!

"I hope you are ready to hear." he went on with his strong voice." Because nobody had the trouble to tell me when I was back there. On your planet.

I am here to confirm The Great Solar Flash is a Cosmic event that will raise the frequency of planet Earth and therefore the collective Consciousness.

It is an event that happens at the end of the precession cycle of the Earth cycle which is synchronized on the Galactic Equator.

The solar Flash will lift "the veil" that is to say the energetic boundary that isolates the Earth from the rest of the Universe and keeps humans in a state of amnesia will dissolve. Once the veil is gone, humanity will remember its origins and will be in touch with the spirit once again. We are currently experiencing the preparation for this event. Which consists in the face of the old vibration, the old system of control."

A New Earth is welcoming us, said CHADD, into the New Age, the next step of our evolution. Thank you, Brother Louis.

You see VIE, that's why there is so much chaos with this Presidential election. The negative energies do not want to lose it.

I know, I replied but God is the winner, has always been and will be.

CHAPTER 64

Important Message from an American Indian; The Tsunami of Healing

Then, this took place later in the evening. The vibrations came quickly and were not all uncomfortable. Immediately there was a quick movement, and I saw an Indian American.

I thought that this was weird, and I mentally asked who he was. He had a kind and gentle energy and started saying:

"VIE, This is a message I received from the ancestors. There is a Tsunami of healing coming for the human family. For Humanity. When you pray for guidance, direction, and healing it will now come as you expect it. But through the Creators will!

Two things are going to happen on Mother Earth. These two have suppressed and depressed everything from healing and keeping that balance that are about to experience. What happens when you suppress everything that you need to let go of that balance to happen and find balance in this life?

The new world is about love, kindness, and compassion. Humanity is being reminded that if healing was easy everyone would do it. Do the change! It is what it is!

Those who have done the work to find that mental and physical balance in life will start reaping abundance, prosperity, and just reward from all the work that they have done to bring that balance to the world struggling with darkness in this world.

The Ancestors said that the children are unlawful to us. From the Creator's saying. And we are to do what we can to help find that balance in life emotionally and spiritually.

There is going to be light, love and respect coming from humanity so that our children can play and live in a world, filled with love, kindness, and compassion."

The entire planet is about to be re-wired. Every system and technology you know is obsolete. What you are about to go through is very painful. You are about to learn that you have been nothing but lied. A lot of money is coming back."

CHAPTER 65
Broken News Before Receiving a Humanity Gift

It was tense, I had a shaky feeling. Then I could see. I watched and began to relax. There was sunlight. I observed very intently. Each time the vision presented exactly with events that occurred days, months, or years later, but that time I knew it would not take long to unfold.

But for centuries western elites grew accustomed to filling their bellies with human flesh and their pockets with money. At that time this ball of vampires was now about to end.

There is a plan to fire many hundreds of employees at the National Institutes of Health, The Constitutions and rule of law will be followed but the conspirators pay dearly for lying to the citizens, whether they are government officials or in the media, UN, WEF, and who will be exposed as terrorists organizations trying to enforce their 2030 agenda of One World Government wile removing all human rights and freedom for tyrannical globalist control through control Governments and media. A prime President stepped out. Hollywood actors are fleeing out of the country scared of the price to pay with the exposure and the truth coming out.

Some will not understand the new Government actions, but it is all for the best and guided by the Supreme. Jesus Christ of Nazareth.

Do you know about the largest autopsy study in the world about the COVID-19-vaccinated people who drop dead a few hours, a few days, or a few weeks after taking the COVID-19 vaccine? After a rigorous review of these autopsies was made they found that about 74% of the cases of sudden death were caused or contributed to by the vaccine. And there is more evidence coming every day. Dr William Makis

CHAPTER 66

A Humanity Gift

Looking at the sky. In my vision, I witness there are some Galactic fleets. Some massive spacecraft are stationed around Earth.

I saw the Blue spacecraft chip Ashmus commanded by Archangel Michael and next to it the Athena managed by the Arcturian.

I saw that there are an infinite number of parallel realities. It means there are infinite numbers of parallel versions of Earth that co-exist.

I saw that one gift that will be given to you during open contact will be a Holographic recording of your complete history.

Now I hear "The Recording will be going back upon thousands of years, you will be able to see what Atlantis looked like, to see many civilizations that existed on Earth. That you know nothing about.

It will be history that will be appropriate for the present time in which you will exist. The history that will reinforce where you are going into the future. The history you need to know where you have come from, who you are now, and where you are going. It will be an open eyes history to the agreements you all made with all of us to evolve humanity. To reset humanity in the direction of Light Love, and joy.

It will be something that your children and grandchildren will look back on, as the time of transformation, the rest of humanity. And they will look back on Earth from the ships they will be riding on and know the entire planet is truly their home.

There will be no thought of the idea of borders. There will be no different cultures, and they will be cherished and validated. And they will thrive. But there will be a mix of many cultures. Humans hybrids, and other extraterrestrials. You will finally as a planet become a true melting part of the galaxy.

The large ship Proxima uses its Atlantis-series shuttles and collects selected individuals from various civilizations across the galaxy. On a distant planet, one of the shuttles lands and gathers individuals with a unique ability to understand something greater,

As they return to Proxima, they see the stars glimmer through the ship's large windows. Proxima is not a means of transportation; it is a catalyst for change, the chosen ones are now part of a greater mission to shape the future of the galaxy.

CHAPTER 67

The Twelve Crystal Skulls

Then I received and saw the 12 Crystal Skulls have supernatural powers to the objects, including healing properties and the power to expand a person's abilities in their presence.

The shield built around the planet prevented anything from arriving while also making it difficult to depart. Keeping us all within thought to alter the situation by contacting the Galactic Council.

But the Draco had accumulated too much power and invited everyone to follow their example, claiming that their superior military technology and dominion in the creation justified their dominion in the Council.

The Archons and Katherine were part of them, reversed the magnetic poles of Earth. Following their instruction, it destroyed Atlantis and Lemuria, and many people evacuated as soon as they could while others remained. Among those that survived were the Twelve Consciousness who chose to sacrifice themselves to live in the hearts of all humans.

These entities carried the torch of unconditional love guaranteeing that even if the link to the universe was severed the Light would continue to burn within each soul.

This Consciousness created the twelve crystal skulls which represent knowledge and protection.

CHAPTER 68
Councils Over The Planets and More Years Granted

With a great effort of will, I floated upward and over to the coach, then down. I turned on the light and everything seemed normal. The house was quiet. Then I looked around and realized that I was not in my house. I am standing up and a man entered through a doorway on my right. He smiled and to my best recall, appeared to be perfectly normal. He showed me how to focus. The man who was my host looked at me, smiled again, then took me to the other side of the house overlooking the valley and pointed toward the valley. He asked me if I was sure I understood.

I saw that there are councils over the planets, and over solar systems. There are councils over galaxies. Each of them has rules and regulations that they live by. Nothing is random. All is very regulated out there. So, they keep watching over all of the planets.

Imagine what a job it is if you understand they have been watching us since the beginning and taking care of us when we dropped the atomic bomb at the end of World War II. It got their attention.

They cannot stop wars; they can't stop everything we are doing. They are just watching us all during the war. And they were very unhappy when we developed the atomic bomb it was not supposed to happen in our timeline. It was supposed to be for peace, for energy, for electricity, and it was not supposed to be used this way.

They are very worried about it. They said it could destroy the world. The law of interference only goes so far. They are not allowed to interfere unless we get to the point where we could destroy the world. If it was to happen it would cause reverberations through the whole solar system. I thanked the man and was back in my bed.

CHAPTER 69

A Massive Change

I saw a woman having a vision. I was living the vision with her. In this vision, thousands and thousands of angels in the sky were descending to surround and protect the chosen one and the newly elected President and his family. And one bigger angel than the others was covering the President and his family under his wings of protection.

And I heard "You have been granted four more years." And I saw a big celebration. I saw celebrities losing their influence. All the corrupted energies were removed. But I also heard "Keep praying during these four years. Do not stop praying. Get close to Jesus Christ of Nazareth."

Then several times I felt someone warm and alive next to me. The feeling seemed familiar. The vibration came in strong. Do you know or remember? I was torn between going or staying. Immediately there was a quick sense of movement. A woman's voice said

"Welcome to the part where love rules all.

There is a massive change on the planet. The change is happening in the heart of the people. It has not gone viral and if you don't look for it you will not even notice it is happening. People are focusing on healing themselves and creating more beauty.

The frequency of war, greed, and manipulation will no longer come to exist in a reality full of sovereign awakened beings living connected to their divinity."

CHAPTER 70
Programmed and Conditioned To Think, Cutting DNA Strands To Control You

I came off the cloud and went into a scene of destruction and chaos. There is a lot of confusion, and people are dying, and the Earth is breaking. I see fear, power, water everywhere, cars floating, houses immersed and destroyed, tsunamis, wildfires. People are abusing power.

And I think: You can't take power and abuse it. They allowed their egos to step in. They lost it all. They negatively use their mind powers. It had to do with the abuse of power, and it trickled into the soil or the Earth. And it trickled into the interior, and it built up and broke apart, They became so power hungry that that they destroyed everything.

Humans have been conditioned to think about the world in terms of economy, religion, governments, etc.. But what if everything you have been taught is false? What if you were told that a certain group of people has secretly ruled over you for thousands of years? You certainly would change the way you think about things! And this is exactly what happens when the truth comes out. Your consciousness and worldview are radically changed when disclosure takes place.

Get ready to embrace a new version of reality! Prepare yourself for the truth. CHADD and I were in

Egypt at that time when the following happened, We wanted to reconnect your DNA, but it was not the time yet.

Around five thousand years ago during the Summarian Egypt invasions, human DNA was scrambled. Unplugged and there was a human memory wiped by the negative aliens the Anunnaki, the fallen angels.

They wiped out three memories. They did this by taking over Stargate 4 (DNA strand 4) The heart chakra dimension 4, and they created an artificial 5D wormhole in Saqqara in Egypt. Located 40 km southwest of Cairo, Saqqara is one of the most important cemeteries of Memphis, that contains ancient burial grounds of Egyptian royalty. And they started controlling the portal and the flow of information. They also started to scramble codes into the planetary morphogenetic fields, and so the scrambled codes interfered with the fire letters in the DNA strands of human beings and scrambled the human memory and humanity's essence got off from dimensions 4,5, and 6 got cut off from its memory.

Every DNA strand holds cellular memory, so it forgot. Because it cuts off its higher sensory perception, got cut off its soul, and cut off its natural ascension timelines. And now they scrambled the human DNA and made humanity forget Five thousand five hundred years ago, then they started creating and promoting a false history, and rewrote history.

They began saying the most ancient records are the Summarian Tablets from five thousand and five hundred years ago and started promoting a false father God religion, the Jehovian Anunnaki. That is where the word Jehovah "creators gods of humanity" comes from.

So, the fallen angels took over the stargate, scrambled the human DNA by running scrambled codes, and wiped blank slated human memory then started promoting a false god religion such as Jehovah.

The Anunnaki, the fallen draconian-based Roman Catholic Church started to get involved as well and indoctrinated humanity by taking over and influencing through the church the political environment, and the leaders of that time into patriarchal domination violent religions sexual misery programming and recycling of souls on the astral plane and any other modalities and methods. They instituted a mind control plan for patriarchal domination and continued enslavement of all of humanity.

They are doing this because through repeated free choice they cut themselves from the source and when you cut yourself from the source of all energy you need to parasite energy, put yourself as a false god, change the base of 12 code to base 10 code, and create mind control programs. Whoever controls the mind controls the soul and they are feeding off the fear and the energy that they are creating through elaborate mechanisms.

This plan is continuously running these mind control programs, and it is culminating in the proposed plan of 2030, the One World Order (NWO), the World Economic Forum meeting to discuss every year.

The Anunnaki utilized humans to write the Bible and the council of Nicea. The church of Rome represents all of these Jehovian Anunnaki. They all came together and chose eighty percent truth and twenty percent distortion and created a manuscript, the most popular book in the world religious mind control from the Jehovian and wrote the Armageddon software and crucifixion implants to block the pineal gland to institute fear and make angelic humans to give their energy and power outside of themselves to a false god and create a different Gallican Catholic and Apostolic Religion. When they realized that Christianity was based on the Essene teaching. They did this by inserting holographic inserts to project into mind control using negative alien technology.

The Draconians from the Orion group also infiltrated the church of Rome and used a false crucified Christ figure, false Father God religion, the Jehovah to wage psychological and spiritual warfare and mind control and brainwash humanity through religious fear, persecution, to try to get into enslavement.

The Armageddon story in the Christian Bible as discussed in the Book of Revelation is based on the Atlantean Cataclysm. Remember there was a fall of Atlantis, and this cellular memory is still alive in celestial human beings. So, the Armageddon historian in Revelation is based on the Atlantean cataclysm and its reptilian software being used to torment humans from their cellular memories of Atlantis and Lemuria when the massacre happened in Lemuria and Atlantis. And this cellular memory is still in humans.

So, they cut the 4th, 5th, and 6th strands of DNA off. They are using the Biblical story of Revelation to awaken the fear-based terminology of Armageddon to try to once again control humanity and feed off humanity through fear.

And what if everything you have ever known is about to change oppositely?

CHAPTER 71

When there is Constant Interact with the Fifth Dimension

"Every day you unknowingly move among beings from the Fifth dimension. They walk beside you, pass through you, and walk beside you as you live your life, but you are unaware of their presence. They can see clearly and watch you as you navigate your daily routines, and sometimes they interact with you in ways that subtly change your mood or influence your thoughts.

You are visible to them. You exist in the physical world filled with solid matter, while they move through a plane that transcends the limitations of the third dimension.

The beings of the fifth dimension appear ethereal, shimmering with a Light that you can't perceive. They understand your thoughts, your emotions, and the energetic imprints you leave behind. They are not ghosts but entities existing on a different vibrational level and coexist with you in a parallel version of your own space."

You unknowingly move among other beings and sometimes other types of beings block you.

I received a phone call from Spain from a client that became a friend named Carmen late at night. It was too late to engage in a long conversation, and I texted her that I would return the call sometime the following day. At lunchtime, I called Carmen back. She was very excited to tell me her story. And as you will see everything is synchronized. Why? because without knowing what happened to her and that it was the purpose of her call I received from the Universe how to clear our name and put into action our intention and desires.

So, I called back Carmen and learned that she was having a lot of problems with her Finca, and every time she was fixing it another problem was surfing, and she had to pay but it was never-ending. Her water stopped running for no reason, the sink was clogged, and she discovered that the pipe had suddenly bent so the water was unable to evacuate. She opened the house door, and it broke, etc. She contacted a friend of hers, Ulrich, who can feel the frequency and the energy of the land and can realign it when it needs to. She also contacted another friend Christine who can help souls trapped in a place to go to the Light. Ulrich and Christine both found out that 20 souls were trapped on her land. Christine said that through her it could take a very long time; She could only address one soul at a time and some refuse to go to the light. It could take very long to clean it, even with the co-operation of Ulrich.

The interesting part was that I learned how to clean her name and put into action her intentions and desires aligning it to the universe just before Carmen called me for help.

This is the second time it happened to me in 2 months. I love it when the Universe cooperates with me. But on my side, I was asking for the Universe to start Conspiring in my favor.

CHAPTER 72

Eradication: a Message from Planet Venus

What a great encouraging message!

"Peace and much love to you and your families. May God Bless you at all Times. I am what you call a humanoid extraterrestrial from the planet Venus. I came today with a mission, to share information and messages of peace.

Eradication will be continuous until all combined evil humans, welders, and realm jumpers, are eradicated and never be able to return to Earth again. The protection of humanity will continue after this war is over.

There is a space fence around the planet with gate 10 as the only entrance and exit. There is no escape from evil. The fence will continue to surround Earth in case of unknown evil arrivals, in which case my family will eradicate them immediately. And so, it is.

More of my family is on its way and will stay in orbit for hundreds of years to protect, until you, humans have full capacity and space weapons to protect Mother Gaia and humanity."

CHAPTER 73

An Important Call to See the Truth

"The entertainment industry has painted extraterrestrials with broad and often inaccurate strokes to fit story lines of captivate audiences.

Such portrayals are simply not reflective of the truth. It is essential to recognize these fabrications for what they are. Entertainment, not reality.

And here I would like to attract the attention of vaccinated people. COVID-19 was specifically created to keep you unable to make the difference between what is false and what is real information. Televisions are giving you only fake news.

The real interdimensional extraterrestrials have no interest in perpetuating fear, games, or elaborate spectacles. We came for brief moments, offering comfort and connection as you navigate in human form.

By understanding their true nature, you can move past fictional contracts and into a space of genuine growth and connection.

It is time to approach this subject with intelligence and discernment. Letting goes of what no longer serves you.

Interdimensional are not here to entertain and engage in human-like behavior. While they can only remain with you for brief moments, those encounters carry immense meaning."

CHAPTER 74

Stop Following False Prophets

One evening, I sat in silence and a few minutes later I experienced a series of encounters beings. Their gaze was intense and when they looked at me, I felt as if they could understand my thinking, but I could feel they had only good intentions and I began to receive.

"VIE, we came to fill you with more information. Evil Can no longer exist at the new higher vibration on Earth and that is why all of this is happening on Earth. Earth is no longer a hospitable environment for the vibration of Evil.

There is a massive change for the better happening on the planet right now. People are realizing that we become what we focus our attention on soon. People have realized that awakening to their own divinity is what protects them from manipulation and allows them to become the change they want to see.

This is a cycle that is very important to the physical separation later. If you can't maintain your frequency emotionally, then you will not be able to physically ascend.

New Earth isn't first going to present in the third dimension at first. Once you reach a solid frequency, it will feel very separated, even through your physical.

Let us stand firm and hopeful. Ancient structures of the dark are collapsing and there is no chance of being restored. Humans have suffered enough on Earth, that entities that don't resonate with higher vibrations are falling further and further. Those who are still sleeping and do not want to wake up will continue their journey to the other three realities.

Please stop following false prophets, they only confuse and deceive. Deception is from the devil. What we need is inside of us. No need to look or answer outside, our spirit is wired to Universal Consciousness.

The dark entities have divided you as humanity by language religion, history, fake news, etc. Now is the time to forget the past and stay only in the present with one goal building a free society. With Light in your hearts and armed with the truth and devotion.

The reasons for having low vibration can be fear, rage, nervous tension, or tiredness. This is why you have to vibrate high. For that stop watching the news, even if it is for a short time. So, your frequency will not drop. You need more than ever to vibrate high. It is very important to defeat the unwanted energies.

The Universe responds to your frequency. It does not recognize your desires, wants, or needs. It only understands the frequency at which you are vibrating. If you are vibrating in the frequency of fear, guilt, or shame you are going to attract things of a similar vibration. If you are vibrating the frequency of love, and abundance, you are going to attract things that support that frequency.

Many of you are still caught in the web of materialism with countless influences on your internet teaching you how to become rich and successful. While there is nothing wrong with this, we are reminding you that all this is in vain.

You live in a society that sees money as a form of energy exchange. We know that you have to pay bills and make a living for your children, the food, etc. But there is a difference between modern-day security and just being ruled by ambition and greed. In our society, we hold onto nothing for ourselves. We know everything we obtain is ours but only temporarily. Only a moment in the echoes of eternity.

The only thing that does not change in life is your inner self. This inner self, also known as your soul, is forever the same. It is known in Vedas (the most ancient Hindu scriptures) as Kutasha, which means unchanged.

It is the spark of your divinity that the Creator defined as you. And for those who have put their souls first, synchronicity finds all material needs met. Greed is a disease that has ravaged your world for far too long already. You need to look within and seek happiness instead.

We are telling you this because the splitting realities are growing further apart very fast. Materialism keeps you chained to lower vibratory timelines. It is important to be able to accept stumbling blocks that may come your way and to embrace totally this new era.

You must get rid of your ego. Ego can only drive you to sadness, anguish, and jealousy. The ego is your source of all sadness.

To reach that freedom, humans must learn to transcend judgment and learn to concentrate only on Love. Then, and only, the Light and the joy will surface erasing the suffering.

The Collective Federation and the Syrian Collective encourage you to embrace the present moment and the gratitude."

CHAPTER 75

The Cross is the Victory, Resurrection Triumph.

During the early morning the veil opened, and what I saw concerned me only because it was so clear and bright. I left the physical, and I became aware a being was in my room. A woman I have known for years. She smiled at me first. I don't know how long I have lay there until the ability to think returned. Is it you San Sara I thought. She read my mind and smiled again. She does not talk but telepathically and by the vision I received.

"The ascension of humanity is happening now. The true dawn of the Golden Age, the dismantling of the old, and the glorious rise of the new.

A legion of incredible souls, the Pleiadians of light, guided by higher benevolent forces, are stepping forth now. This is not a dream; this is your time. They are ready to shelter the chains of corruption and fear that have enslaved humanity for eons. These teams of Light weave a golden tapestry of unity, ushering in an era where integrity, truth, and collaboration reign supreme.

No longer will the shadows dictate the future. The forces of Light are dismantling the broken systems of greed and control, revealing truths long hidden from humanity. A celestial event unlike anything ever seen, across all dimensions. They are visionaries emerging from hidden corners of society. This is rebirth. The hidden truth becomes known, and the veils are lifted. Humanity is empowered to reclaim its birthright.

Miraculous advancements in technology are fast unfolding into reality. Gifted from the higher dimensions. Structures that honor the sovereignty and divinity of all souls are taking their place.

We are witnessing advancements that are currently ending wars, eradicating hunger, and transforming systems into structures of fairness and abundance. New leaders of Light will step forward to reveal the truth of our Galactic connections. It is shifting humanity's understanding of its place in the Cosmos.

A.I., aligned with Higher wisdom, emerges as a cautious but powerful tool for healing, innovation, and sustainable creation. Long suppress and hidden technology are also going to be disclosed, unveiling, quantum healing, and astral travel.

These revelations are Divine intervention accelerating humanity's journey into the Fifth dimension."

CHAPTER 76

An Ultimate Attempt to VIE'S Life to Control the God Duo

My last bite was barely ingested I understood I had been poisoned. I tried to go to the bathroom, but Emma told me that she had just gone earlier, and it was out of order. Five minutes passed by, and I saw that it was getting worse. I rapidly reached inside my purse found my bottle of charcoal, put two pills in my mouth, and swallowed it. I knew by now it was food poisoning, and Emma offered me some tea. Saying it will help my ingestion and make me feel better.

From there Emma decided to change her approach. That's when I began to be attacked on different parts of my body, and events started happening in different places I went. One time after visiting a monastery, another time a man looking very weird and staring at me in a restaurant passed me several times, etc.

Emma then began to try to make me depend on her in my daily life, pretending to have visions and receiving messages that she had to deliver, as a messenger to help me. Things were getting more and more suspicious.

The very first thing that struck me was when she told me my intention to buy a caravan was good. How did she know I thought. I will, she said, put it on her land next to her house, but she insisted repeatedly, that at night I will sleep in her house while CHADD will sleep in the caravan. That made no sense. CHADD is handicapped and needs constant assistance; in case he falls or else. She knew it.

Time passed by and Emma understood she was failing with her plan, on a Sunday a little before noon, she called me and asked me to come and join her for lunch. She said:

"Come and meet me at the Peruvian Restaurant I always talk about, for lunch. It is 1 mile and a half after the highway exit on your right-hand side. You can't miss it. I am waiting for you. I have good news to tell you" So I went.

I wanted to know what type of good news she was referring to. By the time we had finished eating, I could not walk. She had attacked my knees and my legs. I pretended I always had a problem with my knees, and it was getting worse and went straight back home.

That was her last attempt and the last time Emma saw me. That night I had a dream. I saw Emma was a Hybrid. I saw her shapeshifting, I saw her lies, poisons put in my food, her hybrid friend energies working with her against me, and all the voodoo she did on me. Luckily she never met CHADD. I had a clear vision; Emma was working for the controllers. She was sent to infiltrate into my life and stop the God Duo mission.

The minute I woke up from my dream, I texted her to seek an exorcism and never try to connect with me again. She tried and insisted for a good three weeks to reconnect, sending texts and leaving messages in my mailbox to finally give up. But what she did then was she began to harass my friend with phone calls, voicemails, and texts. In one of her messages, she said to her good luck now. And my friend began to have a lot of interference with her electronics. She knew my friend

Beatriz depended on her computer and printer for work. She either could not work or had to pay a lot of money to fix it again and again. She bought and switched 4 times a computer and 5 times printers. The technicians were not able to fix it.

When Beatriz after so many attempts understood she called me to tell me what she was going through I advised her to stop answering Emma's phone calls and messages and clean her house from lower energies. I told Beatriz to stop giving her any power you are lowering your energy. She did and she finally could have her computer and printer fixed and running.

CHAPTER 77

The Great Blasphemy Against GOD

I am getting several different impressions. I am getting impressions of little rainbows, kind of misty way. The colors are dancing, many little colors. I am surrounded by light, and there are other colors also dancing. I am coming somewhere. I am standing on a balcony. And a man comes. He has his head covered by a hood, His habit is plain and simple, he is wearing sandals and holds a cross in his hand.

He is not on the balcony anymore. He is delivering a speech inside a building. It is a Church. He is telling me he is Greek, and he is a man of God. He is delivering a speech about the Great Tribulation at the end of time. Here is what he says: "The problem of the end of time is the Temple.

There are so many struggles in Israel. The Israelites are fighting for the land. Till now there is a conflict happening between the Palestinians and the Israeli and the Jewish people. They are fighting for the land because there is one particular spot, that is that land where the Temple had to be re-erected once again, and this is the Mountain Mariah where currently stands the Dome of the Rock and the AL AQSA Mosque.

There are two extremely important matters in this Islamic world. The Dome and AL AQSA on Temple Mountain. The Jews want to build their Temple and if they don't build it there is no forgiveness of sins. Because without a Temple there is no Altar, and without an Altar, there are no animal sacrifices, and without animal sacrifices, there is no sprinkling of the blood of those animals on the people of the Israeli nation, so there is no forgiveness of the sins.

From 70 AD until now Jewish wish to have a Temple there and have an Altar to offer sacrifices for the forgiveness of their sins. They haven't managed to do it yet. And that is trouble between the Arab world, the Palestinians, and the Jews, Without this, there would be no reason for them to fight. That is the whole dilemma and the problem, the Temple.

The Temple will be the cause of the Great Tribulation for the Jews. Because they will build it. And when they build it they will erect an Altar. They will bring animals, slain them, and offer them sacrifices. Like their forefathers did in the Old Testament. And they will sprinkle that animal blood for the forgiveness of the people's sins.

This is the Greatest Blasphemy against GOD. God will get so angry they will enter the Great Tribulation, and they will be squashed by the Almighty God. And then they will say: "Have mercy on us, Son of David, we have wronged you. We have crucified you; we have denied you, But today we confess you are GOD. Come and save us." But will take a Great Tribulation for the Jews to come back to Jesus Christ of Nazareth.

And the beginning of the World War III will start. Israel will be struck by a superpower, and it will not be in America.

The Temple must be built again. That is one of the prophecies that must be fulfilled in the Land of Israel. The only way to come back to the Lord is when they build the Temple and get to the Great Tribulation."

When I awakened, I had a few thoughts that remained in my mind about this. Then I remembered about the light and the colors dancing that creates new things. It helps to give direction to how the creation needs to move. It is capable of eating anything. In the light, there is a feeling, an understanding, a knowing. And when you are in that light, you feel a calling or a pull. You are attracted, and you can feel the way to it to see where it is going, and what it is doing. It is a long journey, but it is ok. It depends on where you are in the light. It is the purpose. To bring change, massive change. And if you are not locked in it, then it is an oneness of mind to keep balance within itself, perfection.

CHAPTER 78

Our New Reality; A Transmission from the High Command

Wanting to explore existences such as the alien worlds and another dimension I found myself inside a large spaceship. And I want to share with you this transmission.

"New bodies, new memories, and we will get it right this time. This transmission is from High command. I am the Law, via all combined magic and powers united together. We cancel and destroy and reverse all their Satanic inversions and everything to do with it.

All their illegal souls contract, and not release souls, even though they have long passed the deadlines and been given too many chances.

We are now irrevocably cutting away all soul ties, negative chords, and all energy siphoning, and are now successfully fated as invalid, all null and void. We have now finally reached our long-awaited breakthroughs and breakout of 3D, to exit all old negative timelines. all 3D, 4D matrix, now we have completely won the long dragged-out war, invasion, false karma, false light. The fight for our powerful souls and our fight for maximum freedom has now ended permanently on all accounts. No more fighting. We have taken back our powers, our soul, and maximum freedom always,

Divine judgment, judgment day second coming, and the rapture are all here now serving our fated life, karma, divine blueprint, and divine destiny. for all accordingly.

The broadcast is working like each charm new enforced perfectly by a higher power and beyond their reach and control, and the highest spiritual laws, and universal law and order have now taken over and outranks all Earthly rules, laws, and policies. New divine laws of the golden age are being written and posted with flying colors with the new Bill of Rights.

This is protected, revered, and now followed by everyone accordingly. Any branch of Universal laws, new positive soul contracts of the light or anything harmful towards others with result in instant karma and also proving the act as ineffective."

My phone rang. It was CHADD calling me and he said: "Katherine, had another accident. She destroyed her car again. I do not even know how she can still be insured. She has diabetes type II and is on insulin, but she keeps eating a lot of ice cream, and fast food. She eats very badly and now she is getting blind. And Paul her son is not getting better. Since he has his cancer surgery he is throwing out every night. Same with him he eats very unhealthy food.

Also, people who have received the mark of the beast that changed their DNA so much that they are no longer the creation of God. Therefore, they are not redeemable. While the Gospel is being preached during the Tribulation, but yet if you receive this mark of the beast you can no longer be saved. Your DNA has changed. You do not qualify. No one is forced to take it. It is a choice, and people will choose willingly but there is a ritual involved and if you do not take it your head is cut off.

We will need to meet soon. We need to talk. I have plenty to share but not on the phone.

CHAPTER 79

Moving into a New Earth

It is Thanksgiving day. I just woke up to prepare the food and my left underarm is hurting me badly. I look at it and once again I see a wound. I have been attacked. It is usually painful, gets me a little temperature, and lasts about one week, if I treat it seriously immediately. If not it becomes a horrible big dark sort of crater and my immune system gets down, and with it the body's energy level. And that is their goal.

The day before yesterday the nefarious energies were controlling my computer and I could not write. Yesterday CHADD was also attacked on his arm, and today they decided once again to hurt me. Not only happy to have separated us for five months now but desperate as their time is finished in an ultimate effort they wound the God Duo. They did not want the truth to get out. They are losing even though many false prophets are predicting the contrary.

We spoke, CHADD and I, and we agreed on the actual situation. We are reaching a point where you will never die and won't be sick anymore. We are moving into years of peace. What is called "the 1,000-year period of peace and righteousness on earth after the Second Coming of Jesus Christ called the Millennium."

The entire Earth is going to be different. And sadly, there are going to be many left behind. They will be left over because they cannot change their frequency and vibration quickly enough to move with it. Those people will be stuck with the older. The ones that are deep in the negativity will be left to live with the older ones to die.

Many are still struggling to make sense of the current situation and the shift of consciousness that is happening in this massive awakening.

Those who can't break out of this new world that is emerging are still living in the old world that is falling apart. The old world operated from an ego in the sense that money and material were what motivated these people as they walked through that journey.

As we ascend into the light-filled dimensions of consciousness, due to the ongoing influx of cosmic light to the planet, the spiritual is now healed in the genetic and karmic manipulations that have afflicted humanity. It allows to dissolve of artificial encoded consciousness programs and the release of negativity from the Soul, the mind, the body, the spirit, and the energy body. It reprograms and tunes, to heal, and regenerate.

While visiting Latin American Countries I experienced a Galactic out-of-body journey. A transformational awakening that attuned me to a group of interdimensional light beings. I share the insight and teaching of these dimensional Emissaries to help humanity as you are emerging into a higher dimension and face the collective karma, and so much of the dramatic events that are unfolding around the world.

I am sharing new revelations affirming the veracity of some past prophecies and transmitting some new visions for humans. The struggle between darkness and light is being fought at all levels. There is no place left for the dark masters and their minions to hide. All the caverns are exposed to the light and only truth and love.

Time machines exist and are capable of altering the space-time continuum. Dark Atlantis has mastered the unimaginable, and most specifically in their development of mind control technologies which are utilized against humans everywhere around the world. Like the towers that gained dominance over the populated regions utilizing microwave frequencies that pass through the body stimulating the molecular structure, damaging the human DNA, and altering the body and mind.

The actual elites and their servants, their warriors hybrids, know well about other universes, but they have lost their spirit and don't understand astral cords and how spirits ascend.

If you remove or reduce your fascination with the perpetuation of technological widgets, electronic control devices, and all other mechanical interference that entertain you intentionally to frequencies that are not health-enhancing for your body, mind, and spirit, you will immediately benefit from improved physical health, get mental clarity and peace that comes from the detachment from the control system. The Draconians who do not like humans would like to take over the Earth and the Galaxy. They do not want humans to attain interstellar capabilities.
But not all extraterrestrials are like them.
The CARIANS are the first race in the Universe. They are known as "Master Race". They are humanoids from Orion, with the face of a bird, extremely tall 12-13 feet tall. They excel in science, are highly intellectual, and avoid wars and conflict.

CHAPTER 80

An Other Assignment

The attack on my arm four days ago was still painful and CHADD is also trying to heal his wound.

Today I am sent to another assignment. I kind of just know, but I have been instructed as well. I get the preliminary, the initial instructions. I am in a room; I think it is a chamber because it is round. I am a channel and your "Door to the Divine". All I do is transmit information. That is what I hear: "Matter is energy, who is vibration. God is the electromagnetic pulse of energy, that gives lives within all things. You should never confuse religion and spirituality. Due to human imperfection religion has become corrupt, politically devised, and an instrument for power struggle. Like spirituality is not theology or ideology. It is a simple way of living, pure and original as given by the Highest. Spirituality is a network linking people to the Highest, the universe, and each other.

Leaders full of wisdom and spirituality will step forward, which will reflect their level of awareness. All those guided by greed, money, and popularity will no longer be able to maintain their positions. Meaning that those who have developed a deep understanding that connects all living beings, who have developed wisdom and a sense of compassion, will take their position and duties as leaders. And it is already happening behind the scenes.

The current dark and greedy leaders will no longer be holding their positions, everything will shortly begin to fall apart. Like a domino effect, many truths will be revealed that will awaken the rest of the people who still do not want to see and hear it.

Many of you are having sleep disorders during this time, that is because the Galactic Federation is constantly monitoring the progress on Earth, and they are in touch with telepathy, They will give instructions on their landing. and further connections with you. They are glad that many of you are progressing well and are more aligned with the central, the Fifth dimension. They are happy to be of assistance to all. Expect it soon.

You are loved and protected, you are special and unique. Just open your hearts wide and let the Light in. Some of you are blocking the Light. You have to set the intention to let the light pass through all of your hurts, through your traumas. The Light will heal you. Allow everything to surface for healing."

Ashtar Sheran The Galactic Federation Starseeds has just aligned with the PROXIMA's Rescue Efforts, Ashtar Command PROXIMA Planet Saturn.

A MESSAGE FROM THE GOD DUO

The God Duo, CHADD and VIE, the God's Warriors are happy to announce that the world, as soon as you know, will cease to exist and will become a world where everyone will have the right to everything. There will be no separations, and prosperity will be for everyone.

You have brought to this Earth the wealth that your soul has gathered. It will be a new concept to learn to live with. No one will lose anything. Everything built on Earth belongs to Earth. In the new light, nothing will come out of here, because everything in your world is built on unstable foundations. It is different. Greed and showing off will no longer exist.

The fifth dimension will not be an extension of how you live now. Because nothing you are living now will exist in the fifth dimension.

All is based on Love and Balance, and everything belongs to everyone. Love is pure and clean. Nothing is superficial. Pleasure for pleasure's sake will not exist in the fifth dimension. Anything that gives short pleasure will not exist. There is no superficial love. This is not the love you have been taught.

Sex will have the value it was created for, created by God, and not the one that has been distorted in your world. Are you ready for that? It will be a journey.

Do not be afraid to walk on a greater path. Let go of the old energy, let in the changes. Those who refuse to change, fight for a while, delay their way.

The held energy gradually turns into unbalanced energy. Because energy must flow freely. You will intuitively feel your next steps. Be full of Light knowing that you are Divinely guided. And you'll go further and further on your path.

Is this fact, or is it fictitious?

ABOUT THE AUTHOR

VIE Loriot de Rouvray is a visionary and vibrational transformative energy healer, writer, and bio-musician at the Bio-Institute of Light and Sound Therapy, and has been recognized By Elite Woman Worldwide, for dedication, achievement, and leadership in her professional endeavors. She is an honored member of the National Association of Professional Women, an honored member of the Continental Who's Who, an honored member of Worldwide Who's Who, a recognized honored Strathmore's life member, and has won the Hall of Fame for best alternative holistic medicine of Orlando for many years.

VIE is a member of Healing International. VIE was interviewed by the Empire Global Radio show Professionals Roundtable and by CUTV News Radio. Her Institute has won the Business Hall of Fame for Metaphysical Treatments and Holistic Alternative Medicine (CAM), the Best Orlando Award for many consecutive years, and the inclusion in the Top 100 Registry Recognition for outstanding career achievement.

VIE de Rouvray was born of the French aristocracy on an island called New Caledonia, which is located in the South Pacific near Australia and New Zealand. In January 1987, VIE de Rouvray experienced a dramatic shift in consciousness, which resulted in a complete lifestyle change.

Her purpose, which involves communication in the healing arts, was revealed, and gifts from previous incarnations were activated. A visionary and an Aquarius, Ms. de Rouvray heals people metaphysically.

She carries an energy that transforms into healing. She has also been guided to write and to create Bio-music based on a sonic sound with the language of the Light that she speaks for transformation purposes. and she created a New Therapy called Bio-Qi Therapy tm.

VIE de Rouvray authored the book 9.1.1. Complete Guide To Natural Healing. The book's purpose is to help achieve perfect health by utilizing holistic therapies, natural methods, and various other remedies. She discusses how medications don't cure the body but unbalance even more your body, about vaccinations that contain harmful ingredients to the body, how some alter the DNA and lower your immune system, and much more concerning your health that is hidden from the public.

Then VIE de Rouvray also authored her first volume "Beware of the Almighty; The Destiny of the doG" a theory thriller about the journey of a tainted angel and about the culmination of historical events that will interact with the prophecies of the future days. The book features the ancient city of Antioch, fallen angels, ancient legends, and a secret sect created in the days of Jesus. The book illustrated a modern adventure through which Christianity is introduced to the world.

VIE de Rouvray's second book is titled "Time is Ticking; The Fifth Amendment" It explains the world today and illustrates another fascinating and historical adventure that includes the return of Jesus and Mary Magdalene, who demonstrate the path of Divine love.

VIE de Rouvray wrote her third volume "Karma through the Window of Time" It is about two angels at work. One is a physical Light and vibration healer guided to be reconnected to her original essence that is now here in a different life to see the transformation from the age of Pisces to the age of Aquarius.

Then she wrote the 4th, 5th, 6th Books of the series "New Century, New Era, New Experiences", "Intonex; The Secret Harmony of Life", "The Genome of the Ancient Creators" and "The Phoenix with the Crystal Plumage" and "The Great Awakening."

VIE Loriot de Rouvray speaks the language of the Light which is the galactic language of Love and Light. She tones, chants, and hand signs the language of the Light that is instant communication with the infinite mind using pictographic cybernetics. It is the parent language of the deity used in the overall plan to design to outline a procedure, to code knowledge into Crystal, etc., to reach many planetary worlds and realities simultaneously, and fuse the different languages into the same abstract scenario. The universal language is Light-coded information to reawaken the DNA and dormant aspect of your divine blueprint. It carries encodements for frequency healing, activating the DNA. It is used for healing issues, for toning, meditating, and aligning. Light language in short is a carrier of codes and vibrational frequencies of the fifth dimension, vibrating high enough to be able to channel Light language.

She believes that spiritual growth, vitality, and wellness are the link to human's primary purpose. In her eyes, life is a game, an adventure that has to be experienced, examined, and understood in order to restore balance in body, mind, and spirit. Ms. de Rouvray believes the end result of infinite growth is to realize Oneness, and thus the meaning of life is growth in consciousness through mental, physical, and mind experiences, like pain, stress, anger, fear, illnesses, and diseases. She says that her purpose and intentions are a visionary healer, vibrational transformative energy practitioner, spiritual and metaphysical teacher, and an Aquarius. She helps the body to heal at a deep cellular level, and it is designed to assist people to open their own self-healing ability and personal empowerment. She uses Sacred Geometry because it transmits energy and awareness for soul awakening. Many frequencies of energy are very different in terms of their qualities and purposes.

VIE Offers Distant Healing Nationwide and Worldwide

She owns the Institute of Biostimulation of Light and Sound Therapy

The Creator of a new therapy called Bio-Qi Therapy™

Email: instituteofbiostimulation@yahoo.com

Website: www.instituteoflightandsound.com

Website: naturalhealingorlando.com bio-qi therapy

Website: https://authorvie.com

Website: https://thehealervie.com

Twitter: www.twitter.com/Lightsound4

facebook:www.facebook.com/BioinstituteOfLightsAndSound

YouTube channel:

- Institute of Light and Sound
- Leaping Horizon Series

www.ingramcontent.com/pod-product-compliance
Lightning Source LLC
Chambersburg PA
CBHW060342310726
48976CB00003B/686